THE
RUSSIAN
REVOLUTION

THE FALL OF THE TSARS AND
THE RISE OF COMMUNISM

EDITED BY
RUSSELL TRENTON

Britannica®
Educational Publishing
IN ASSOCIATION WITH
ROSEN
EDUCATIONAL SERVICES

Published in 2016 by Britannica Educational Publishing (a trademark of Encyclopædia Britannica, Inc.) in association with The Rosen Publishing Group, Inc. 29 East 21st Street, New York, NY 10010

Distributed exclusively by Rosen Publishing.
To see additional Britannica Educational Publishing titles, go to rosenpublishing.com.

First Edition

Britannica Educational Publishing
J.E. Luebering: Director, Core Reference Group
Anthony L. Green: Editor, Compton's by Britannica

Rosen Publishing
Kathy Campbell: Senior Editor
Nelson Sá: Art Director
Nicole Russo: Designer
Cindy Reiman: Photography Manager
Introduction and supplementary material by Russell Trenton

Library of Congress Cataloging-in-Publication Data

The Russian Revolution: the fall of the tsars and the rise of Communism/edited by Russell Trenton.
    pages cm.—(The age of revolution)
Includes bibliographical references and index.
ISBN 978-1-68048-032-0 (library bound)
1. Soviet Union—History—Revolution, 1917-1921—Juvenile literature. I. Trenton, Russell, editor.
DK265.R957 2015
947.084'1—dc23
                                                                                    2014043860

Manufactured in the United States of America

Photo credits: Cover, pp. 1, 36, 60 Print Collector/Hulton Archive/Getty Images; pp. vi–vii © Photos.com/Thinkstock; p. 2 DEA/M. Seemuller/De Agostini/Getty Images; pp. 7, 50, 67, 104, 122 Heritage Images/Hulton Archive/Getty Images; p. 8 Album/Prisma/SuperStock; p. 14 Fine Art Images/ SuperStock; p. 21 FotoSoyuz/Hulton Archive/Getty Images; p. 33 Apic/Hulton Archive/Getty Images; pp. 39, 41 Universal Images Group/Getty Images; p. 48 DEA Picture Library/Getty Images; p. 73 Imagno/Hulton Archive/Getty Images; p. 76 Keystone/Hulton Archive/Getty Images; p. 79 Mondadori/ Getty Images; pp. 80–81, 83, 94 Sovfoto/Universal Images Group/Getty Images; p. 89 Topical Press Agency/Hulton Archive/Getty Images; p. 95 Laski Collection/Hulton Archive/Getty Images; p. 109 Private Collection/Calmann & King Ltd/Bridgeman Images; p. 111 Private Collection/Bridgeman Images; p. 114 © Heritage Image Partnership Ltd/Alamy; pp. 116–117 State K. Savitsky Art Museum, Pensa/Bridgeman Images; p. 120 © AP Images; p. 124 Universal History Archive/UIG/Getty Images; p. 129 Keystone-France/Gamma-Keystone/Getty Images.

CONTENTS

CONTENTS

CONTENTS

The roots of the Russian Revolution of 1917 ran deep. Russia had suffered under an extremely oppressive form of government for centuries under the rule of the tsars and tsarinas (emperors and empresses). From 1613 until the Russian Revolution, Russia was ruled by tsars and tsarinas of the Romanov Dynasty. All together there were 18 Romanov rulers. The best-known members of the dynasty were Peter I the Great, Catherine II the Great, Alexander I, Nicholas I, Alexander II, Alexander III, and Nicholas II. The dynasty ended with the abdication of Tsar Nicholas II in 1917 during the Russian Revolution and the eventual execution of his family. The account of the Russian Revolution related in the pages of this book highlights the major causes, participants, events, and consequences of the civil war. In addition, it places the revolution in the larger historical and international context, imparting

an indispensable understanding of the Russian cultural, societal, and political realms of today.

During the 19th century the country was filled with movements for political liberalization. In the long run there were several revolutions, not one. The first rebellion, known

VLADIMIR LENIN, LEADER OF THE BOLSHEVIKS AND A POWERFUL ORATOR, ADDRESSES A MOSCOW CROWD DURING THE RUSSIAN REVOLUTION OF 1917.

as the Decembrist uprising, took place in December 1825. Members of the upper classes, including many former soldiers, staged a revolt after the death of the tsar, Alexander I. The revolt failed, but it provided an inspiration to succeeding generations of dissidents.

The next revolution took place in 1905, after the Russo-Japanese War, which Russia lost. It appeared briefly that public discontent would force Tsar Nicholas II to establish a constitutional monarchy. Such a change, however, would not have satisfied either the tsar or his opponents. Radical revolutionaries continued to fight for a democratic republic, and the tsar wanted to retain his control of the peasants.

The next two revolutions were successful. They occurred during World War I (1914–18), when Russian military forces were hard-pressed by the Germans. The March Revolution of 1917 led to the abdication of Nicholas and the installation of a provisional government. The leader of this government was Aleksandr Kerensky (1881–1970), who was eventually forced from power.

The last revolution took place in November 1917. (Because the date was in October on the old Russian calendar, it is usually called the October, or Octobrist, Revolution. Russia adopted the Western, or Gregorian, calendar in February 1918.) It brought to power the Bolshevik wing of the Communist Party, led by Vladimir Lenin (1870–1924). The Bolsheviks established the Union of Soviet Socialist Republics under the dictatorship of the Communist Party. In the end Lenin and his followers established a regime that was more rigidly tyrannical than that of any tsar.

In the fall of 1915, as World War I raged, Tsar Nicholas had taken command of Russian armies in the field. This left a power vacuum in St. Petersburg (called Petrograd from 1914 to 1924), the capital. The collapse of the government suddenly came in March (February, old calendar) 1917. Food riots, strikes, and war protests turned into mass demonstrations. The army refused to fire on the demonstrators. A Soviet (or council) of Workers' and Soldiers' Deputies was elected, and it formed a provisional government on March 14. The next day Nicholas abdicated.

The provisional government was a coalition of factions representing divergent points of view. Some leaders wanted withdrawal from the war and immediate economic reforms, with guarantees of political liberty. Others, including Kerensky, wanted to continue the war and postpone all reforms until the conflict was finished. No compromise seemed workable. Meanwhile, Lenin—the revolutionary genius—arrived by train from Switzerland. He had been put on a sealed train by the Germans, who hoped that he would influence Russia to leave the war. This story has been well told by American scholar Edmund Wilson in his book *To the Finland Station* (1940).

Lenin's slogan was "All power to the Soviets!" He used this slogan to undermine the provisional government. He demanded peace at once, immediate land reform, workers' control of factories, and self-determination for the non-Russian peoples. Once in power, he turned his back on all programs of reform, but he kept his promise to take Russia out of World War I.

It was Kerensky's persistence in fighting the war that undid the provisional government, though other factors contributed. The Bolsheviks, led by Lenin, undermined the war effort with propaganda among the soldiers. The government attempted to take action against Lenin, but he went into hiding in Finland. Kerensky tried to reinforce his authority by calling a state conference in Moscow. The Bolsheviks were not represented, but the conference was so divided that it could achieve nothing. A conservative revolt led by General Lavr Georgiyevich Kornilov was put down.

Kornilov's failed revolt was a turning point in the revolution. It became clear that there were not two, but three, opposing forces in the government: the conservatives, the Social Democrats, and Lenin's followers. To Kornilov, the enemy was socialism, personified by Kerensky. To Kerensky, the conservatives represented counterrevolution. Both factions despised and underrated Lenin. To Lenin, Kerensky was as much of an enemy as Nicholas II. The defeat of Kornilov and the exhaustion of the provisional government gave Lenin the chance he had been waiting for.

The leading characters of the next phase of revolution were Lenin and Communist agitator Leon Trotsky. Kerensky seemed unable to take action against the military preparations of the Bolsheviks, who were distributing arms, subverting the army, and appointing supporters as commissars of military units. On the night of November 6–7 (October 24–25, old calendar), 1917, the Bolsheviks acted. By the next evening the capital was in their hands, though fighting in Moscow went on for several days. Soon the Bolsheviks had installed their own general as commander in chief of the armed forces.

When the Second All-Russian Congress of Soviets met in the capital immediately following the Bolshevik coup, most members of other Socialist parties walked out, leaving the impression that Lenin's party best represented the interests of workers, farmers, and soldiers. The congress called upon all parties participating in World War I to negotiate immediate peace. It also abolished all private ownership of land in Russia and took all property of the imperial family and the church. The eight-hour workday was made compulsory, and factory workers were given the right to supervise their enterprises.

Kerensky had earlier planned an election for the end of the month, and Lenin let it go ahead. The results gave the Bolsheviks a distinct minority in the Constituent Assembly. Lenin then appealed over the head of the assembly to the people, claiming the workers' councils (the soviets) represented "a higher form of democratic principle." By January 1918 the assembly was completely demoralized, and it ceased to function.

Meanwhile, Lenin had to deal with the war. Calls for a negotiated peace failed. Lenin then bargained directly with the Germans. Faced with a crippling loss of territory or the collapse of his government, he chose the former. Trotsky headed the Soviet delegation that signed a peace treaty at Brest-Litovsk, in what is now Belarus, on March 3, 1918. Under its terms Russia lost Ukraine, its Polish and Baltic provinces, and Finland. The treaty was effectively annulled by Germany's defeat in November 1918, and the Soviet Union eventually regained all the territory except Finland and Poland.

At the time that the Congress of Soviets met to approve the treaty, the Bolsheviks changed their name to the Russian Communist Party. The treaty had negative effects for Lenin. Opponents from different Russian factions were united by their opposition to it. Patriotic indignation at the betrayal of Russia to Germany quickly surfaced, even in the army. This division between the Communists and their opponents led to a civil war that lasted until late 1920. Trotsky was appointed commissar for war.

Lenin's government, which had relocated to the Kremlin in Moscow, was determined to get rid of all opposition. All non-Bolshevik Socialist factions were driven out of the workers' councils, and they were forbidden to engage in political activity. In retaliation, Lenin was shot and seriously wounded.

The government responded by proclaiming a campaign of "Red Terror," which included shooting hostages and giving the secret police (the Cheka) the power to arrest, try, and execute suspects. Because the Communists feared that Tsar Nicholas might be liberated, he and his family were murdered at Yekaterinburg on the night of July 16–17, 1918.

Although surrounded on all sides by enemies, the Communists had the advantage of controlling the heartland of Russia. Trotsky's Red Army was able to plan operations and move men more easily than its enemies, whose bases were on the fringes and who were cut off from each other. Although all the enemies wanted to destroy the Moscow government, they were not united in other objectives. For example, if the Ukrainians, who simply wanted independence, had won it, they probably would not have continued to fight on behalf of those opposed to the government.

Trotsky managed to take an army that had once been demoralized by Bolshevik propaganda and turn it into an effective fighting force. He used former tsarist officers whose training and experience were too valuable to be ignored. The rigid discipline of the Communist Party helped to raise morale. By 1919 the Red Army had become a much better fighting force than its anticommunist opponents, who were collectively referred to as the Whites. A large part of the peasantry disliked the Communists, but they saw no point in supporting the Whites, who they feared would restore the monarchy. The industrial workers entertained no hope from the Whites, who had shown no understanding of city workers.

After the civil war ended in 1920, the only threat to the Communist government came from the Kronshtadt Rebellion of 1921. Strikes in St. Petersburg led to demonstrations demanding the release of Socialists from prison. In March a mutiny broke out at the nearby naval base of Kronshtadt. The sailors demanded political freedom and the end of the dictatorship of the Communist Party. Lenin, whose chief goal had always been political power, refused any concessions. Trotsky led a force that crushed the mutineers.

Lenin went far to allay economic discontent by advocating such policies as affirming the rights of the peasants to own land, by reducing taxes, and by permitting a certain amount of private enterprise in his New Economic Policy. But in politics he was rigid. No opinions other than those sanctioned by the Communist Party were allowed. The party itself was controlled by its Central Committee and increasingly by smaller units. Effective control passed finally to the secretariat of the party.

When Lenin died in 1924, power passed to the first secretary of the party, Joseph Stalin. Under him still one more revolution took place: the centralization of all political and economic power in his hands and the transformation of the Soviet Union into a completely totalitarian state.

Stalinism, the theory and practice of communism in the Soviet Union under Stalin, was notorious for its totalitarianism, its widespread use of terror, and its "cult of personality"—its portrayal of Stalin as an infallible leader and universal genius. Stalin used the Soviet secret police to arrest anyone who might oppose his rule. Not fewer than 5 million people from all walks of life were executed, imprisoned, or sent to labor camps in Siberia. In the 1930s Stalin staged a series of "show trials" in which thousands of prominent individuals were convicted on false charges of treason and executed.

In pursuit of his policy of "socialism in one country"—the idea that the Soviet Union should transform itself into a major industrial and military power before attempting to export Communist revolution abroad—Stalin forced peasant farmers to work on large agricultural collectives and undertook a program of rapid industrialization. The collectivization of agriculture resulted in the death by starvation of several million people.

The Russian Revolution: The Fall of the Tsars and the Rise of Communism relates the circumstances that led to the end of the Romanov Dynasty and Russian aristocracy, the heartrending struggles of the peasants, the violence and bloodshed of the revolution, and the rise of the new social order and its far-reaching consequences that continue to be felt to this very day.

RUSSIA IN THE 19TH CENTURY

At the beginning of the 19th century, Russian foreign policy was essentially concentrated on the three western neighbour countries with which it had been preoccupied since the 16th century: Sweden, Poland, and Turkey. The policy toward these countries also determined Russian relations with France, Austria, and Great Britain.

HOSTILITIES UNDER ALEXANDER I AND NICHOLAS I

Russo-Swedish relations were settled during the Napoleonic era. When Napoleon met with Alexander I (reigned 1801–25) at Tilsit

THE RUSSIAN REVOLUTION
THE FALL OF THE TSARS AND THE RISE OF COMMUNISM

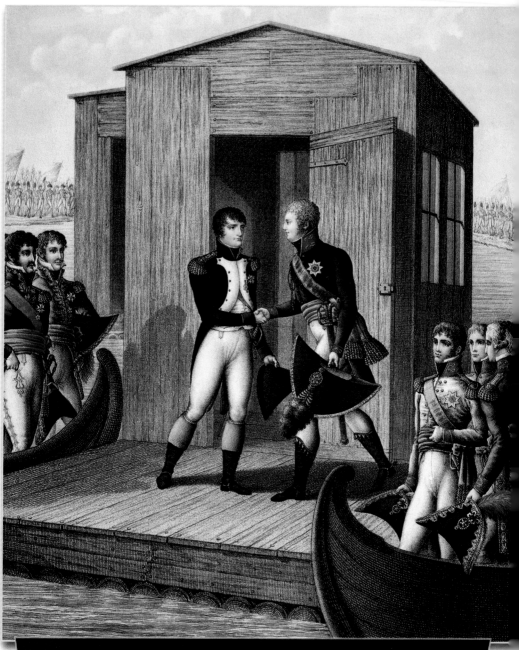

ALEXANDER I (RIGHT) AND NAPOLEON BONAPARTE OF FRANCE MET ON JUNE 25, 1807, ON A RAFT IN THE MIDDLE OF THE NIEMEN OFF TILSIT TO SIGN AN ALLIANCE. ALEXANDER I PROMISED TO BREAK WITH ENGLAND, AMONG OTHER CONDITIONS, AND NAPOLEON GAVE ALEXANDER LIBERTY TO EXPAND AT THE EXPENSE OF SWEDEN AND TURKEY.

(now Sovetsk) in 1807, he gave the latter a free hand to proceed against Sweden. After two years of war, in which the Russians did not always fare well, the Swedish government ceded Finland to the tsar in 1809. Alexander became grand duke of Finland, but Finland was not incorporated into the Russian Empire, and its institutions were fully respected. In 1810, when Napoleon's former marshal, Jean-Baptiste Bernadotte, was elected heir to the Swedish throne, he showed no hostility toward Russia. In 1812 he made an agreement recognizing the tsar's position in Finland in return for the promise of Russian support in his aim to annex Norway from Denmark. Bernadotte achieved this in the Treaty of Kiel (January 14, 1814), and thereafter the relations between Russia and Sweden, now a small and peaceful state, were not seriously troubled.

Alexander I, influenced by his Polish friend Prince Adam Czartoryski, had plans for the liberation and unity of Poland, which had ceased to exist as a state in the 18th century, when it was partitioned among Russia, Prussia, and Austria. After his defeat by Napoleon in 1805, Alexander abandoned those plans in favour of an alliance with Prussia. In 1807 Napoleon established a dependency called the Grand Duchy of Warsaw and in 1809 increased its territory at the expense of Austria. Alexander's attempts to win the Poles to his side in 1811 and to persuade Austria to make concessions to them failed; when Napoleon invaded Russia in 1812, he had 100,000 first-class Polish troops fighting for him. After Napoleon's defeat, Alexander was not vindictive. He protected the Poles against the demands of Russian nationalists who wanted revenge and sought once more to create a large Polish kingdom comprising the territories annexed by Russia and Prussia in the partitions of the 18th century. He was opposed at the Congress of Vienna in 1814–15 by Austria and Britain; the ensuing kingdom of Poland, which, though nominally autonomous, was to be in permanent union with the Russian Empire, consisted of only part of the Prussian and Russian conquests.

Alexander was popular in Poland for a time after 1815. But real reconciliation between Poles and Russians was made impossible by their competing claims for the borderlands, which had belonged to the former grand duchy of Lithuania. The majority of the population of this region was Belarusian, Ukrainian, or Lithuanian; its commercial class was Jewish; and its upper classes and culture were Polish. Neither Russians nor Poles considered Belarusians, Ukrainians, or Lithuanians to make up their own nations, entitled to decide their own fates: the question was whether Lithuania was to be Polish or Russian. Russians could argue that most of Lithuania had been part of "the Russian land" until the 14th century, and the Poles that it had been Polish since the 16th. Alexander had some sympathy for the Polish point of view and allowed the Poles to hope that he would reunite these lands with Poland, but the effective political forces in Russia were strongly opposed to any change. The disappointment of Polish hopes for Lithuania was probably the most important single cause of the growing tension between Warsaw and St. Petersburg in the late 1820s, which culminated in the revolt of the Poles in November 1830 and the war of 1831 between Polish and Russian armies. It ended in the defeat of the Poles and the exile of thousands of political leaders and soldiers to western Europe. Poland's constitution and thus its autonomy were abrogated, and there began a policy of Russification of Poland.

International reactions to the Russo-Polish war were of some importance. Although the governments of France and Britain had failed to come to the aid of Poland during the war, there was much sympathy for the Poles in these countries;

nonetheless, sympathy alone was not sufficient to influence Russian actions. On the other hand, the governments of Prussia and Austria strongly supported Russia. It is arguable that the cooperation among the three monarchies, which continued over the next two decades and was revived from time to time later in the century, had less to do with their eloquently proclaimed loyalty to monarchical government than with their common interest in suppressing the Poles.

Turkey had long been the main object of Russian territorial expansion; through a certain inertia of tradition, the Turkish policy had become almost automatic. It was to some extent reinforced by religious motives—by the romantic desire to liberate Constantinople (Istanbul), the holy city of Orthodoxy—but more important in the second half of the 19th century was the desire to assure the exit of Russian grain exports through the Black Sea. During certain periods, Russia sought to dominate Turkey as a powerful ally; this was its policy from 1798 to 1806 and again from 1832 to 1853. When this policy was successful, Russia supported the integrity of the Ottoman Empire and made no territorial demands. When it was not successful, Russia sought to undermine Turkey by supporting rebellious Balkan peoples or, more directly, by war: this was the case in 1806–12, 1828–29, and 1853–56.

The periods of cooperation were more profitable for Russia than those of conflict. During the first period, a promising foothold was established in the Ionian Islands, which had to be abandoned after the Treaty of Tilsit. During the second period of cooperation, Russia achieved a great success with the 1833 Treaty of Hünkâr İskelesi, which in effect opened the Black Sea straits to Russian warships. Russia achieved a more limited but more durable gain by the Straits Convention of 1841, signed by all the great powers and by Turkey, which forbade the passage of foreign warships through either the Dardanelles or the Bosporus as long as Turkey was at peace, thus protecting Russia's position in the Black Sea unless it was itself at war with Turkey.

In the periods of hostility between Russia and Turkey, the main object of Russian expansion was the area later known as Romania—the Danubian principalities of Moldavia and Walachia. In 1812 Moldavia was partitioned between Russia and Turkey: the eastern half, under the name of Bessarabia, was annexed to Russia. In the war of 1828–29, Russian armies marched through the principalities and afterward remained in occupation until 1834. In 1848 the Russians returned, with Turkish approval, to suppress the revolution that had broken out in Bucharest. It appeared to be only a matter of time before the two Romanian principalities were wholly annexed to Russia. This did not occur, however, because of Russia's defeat in the Crimean War.

The Crimean War (1853–56) pitted Russia against Great Britain, France, and Turkey. It arose from a series of misunderstandings and diplomatic errors among the powers in their conflict of interests in the Middle East, particularly over Turkish affairs. It has been called the unnecessary war. The fact that it was fought in Crimea was due to Austrian diplomacy. In June 1854 the Russian government accepted the Austrian demand that Russian troops be withdrawn from the Danubian principalities, and in August Austrian troops entered. It is arguable whether, on balance, the presence of Austrian troops benefited Russia by preventing French and British forces from marching on Ukraine or whether it damaged Russia by preventing its troops from marching on Istanbul. Tsar Nicholas I (reigned 1825–55) resented the Austrian action as showing

THE BATTLE OF THE CHERNAYA RIVER ON AUGUST 16, 1855, IS DEPICTED BY PAUL LEVERT IN THIS LITHOGRAPH. THE RUSSIANS HOPED TO WIN A VICTORY AT THE BATTLE, ONE OF THE BLOODIEST OF THE CRIMEAN WAR, AND TO HALT THE SIEGE OF SEVASTOPOL, BUT THEIR EFFORTS FAILED.

ingratitude toward the power that had saved Austria from the Hungarian rebels in 1849. When the British and French were unable to attack in the principalities, they decided to send an expedition to Crimea to destroy the Russian naval base at Sevastopol. It was there that the war dragged out its course. The war showed the inefficiency of Russia's top military command and of its system of transport and supply. The Russian armies nevertheless won victories over the Turks in the Caucasus, and the defense of Sevastopol for nearly a year was a brilliant achievement.

ALEXANDER II AND THE ZEMSTVOS

Defeat in Crimea made Russia's lack of modernization clear, and the first step toward modernization was the abolition of serfdom. It seemed to the new tsar, Alexander II (reigned 1855–81), that the dangers to public order of dismantling the existing system, which had deterred Nicholas I from action, were less than the dangers of leaving things as they were. As the tsar said to the nobility of

RUSSIAN SERFS WORK THE LAND IN THIS 19TH-CENTURY PRINT. AFTER THE RUSSIAN DEFEAT IN THE CRIMEAN WAR, REVOLTS AMONG THE PEASANTS INCREASED. IN 1861 ALEXANDER II ISSUED THE EMANCIPATION MANIFESTO, WHICH GAVE THE SERFS PERSONAL LIBERTIES AND PROMISED THEM LAND.

Moscow in March 1856, "It is better to abolish serfdom from above than to wait until the serfs begin to liberate themselves from below." The main work of reform was carried out in the Ministry of the Interior, where the most able officials, headed by the deputy minister Nikolay Milyutin, were resolved to get the best possible terms for the peasants. In this they were assisted by a few progressive landowners, chief among whom was the Slavophile Yury Samarin. But the bulk of the landowning class was determined, if it could not prevent abolition of serfdom, to give the freed peasants as little as possible. The settlement, proclaimed on February 19 (March 3, New Style), 1861, was a compromise. Peasants were freed from servile status, and a procedure was laid down by which they could become owners of land. The government paid the landowners compensation and recovered the cost in annual "redemption payments" from the peasants. The terms were unfavourable to the peasants in many, probably most, cases. In the north, where land was poor, the price of land on which the compensation was based was unduly high; in effect, this served partly to compensate the landowners for the loss of their serfs and also for the loss of the share that they had previously enjoyed of the peasants' earnings from nonagricultural labour. In the south, where land was more valuable, the plots given to the peasants were very small, often less than they had been allowed for their own use when they were serfs.

It is arguable that the main beneficiary of the reform was not the peasant and certainly not the landowner but the state. A new apparatus of government was established to replace the authority of the serf owner. From the *ispravnik*, the chief official of the district, who in 1862 ceased to be elected by the nobility and became an appointed official of the Ministry of the Interior, the official hierarchy now stretched down to the village notary, the most powerful person at this level, who was assisted by an elder elected by an assembly of householders. The lowest effective centre of power was the village commune (*obshchina*), an institution of uncertain origin but great antiquity, which had long had the power to redistribute land for the use of its members and to determine the crop cycle, but which now also became responsible for collecting taxes on behalf of the government.

Further important reforms followed the emancipation. A new system of elected assemblies at the provincial and county levels was introduced in 1864. These assemblies, known as zemstvos, were elected by all classes including the peasants, although the landowning nobility had a disproportionately large share of both the votes and the seats. The zemstvos were empowered to levy taxes and to spend their funds on schools, public health, roads, and other social services, but their scope was limited by the fact that they also had to spend money on some of the tasks of the central government. In 1864 a major judicial reform was completed. Russia received a system of law courts based on European models, with irremovable judges and a proper system of courts of appeal. Justices of the peace, elected by the county zemstvos, were instituted for minor offenses. A properly organized, modern legal profession now arose, and it soon achieved very high standards. The old system of endless delays and judicial corruption rapidly disappeared. There were, however, two important gaps in the system: one was that the Ministry of the Interior had power, regardless of the courts, to banish persons whom it regarded as politically dangerous; the other was that the courts for settling disputes between peasants were maintained and operated on the basis of peasant custom. Their institution by Pavel Dmitriyevich Kiselev (one of Tsar Nicholas I's principal advisers and a leading participant in government administration of the peasantry) in the 1840s had been a well-intentioned reform, but their continuation after emancipation meant that the peasants were still regarded as something less than full citizens.

During the first years of Alexander II's reign there was some demand from a liberal section of the nobility for representative government at the national level—not for full parliamentary rule, still less for a democratic suffrage, but for some sort of consultative assembly in which public issues could be debated and which could put before the emperor the views of at least the educated section of the Russian people. The tsar and his bureaucrats refused to consider this, above all because they saw constitutional reform as a slippery slope that would lead to the disintegration of state and empire and to class war between landowners and peasants. The principle of autocracy must remain sacred; such was the view not only of bureaucrats but also of men such as Nikolay Milyutin and Yury Samarin, both of whom rested their hopes for the progressive reforms they so ardently desired on the unfettered power of the emperor. Their attitude was essentially that of Pavel Stroganov at the beginning of the century, that the sovereign must not have "his arms tied" and so be prevented from realizing "the plans which he had in favour of the nation." The decision against a national assembly in the early 1860s was a negative event of the greatest importance: it deprived Russia of the possibility of public political education such as that which existed, for example, in contemporary Prussia, and it deprived the government of the services of hundreds of talented men.

REVOLUTIONARY ACTIVITIES

The emancipation was received with bitter disappointment by many peasants as well as by the radical intellectuals. The serfs' view of their relationship to the landowners had been traditionally summed up in the phrase, "We are yours, but the land is ours." Now they were being asked to pay for land that they felt was theirs by right. During the 1860s small revolutionary groups began to appear. The outstanding figure was the socialist writer N. G. Chernyshevsky; the extent of his involvement in revolutionary action remains a subject of controversy, but of his influence on generations of young Russians there can be no doubt. In 1861–62 revolutionary leaflets were distributed in St. Petersburg, ranging from the demand for a constituent assembly to a passionate appeal for insurrection. The Polish uprising of 1863 strengthened the forces of repression. An unsuccessful attempt on the tsar's life in 1866 led to a certain predominance of extreme conservatives among Alexander's advisers. Nevertheless, there were still some valuable reforms to come. In 1870 the main cities of Russia were given elected municipal government, and in 1874 a series of military reforms was completed by the establishment of universal military service. This was the work of Dmitry Milyutin, the brother of Nikolay and like him a liberal, who was minister of war from 1861 to 1881.

In the 1870s revolutionary activity revived. Its centre was the university youth, who were increasingly influenced by a variety of socialist ideas derived from Europe but adapted to Russian conditions. These young people saw in the peasantry the main potential for revolutionary action. In 1873–74 hundreds of the youth, including women, "went to the people," invading the countryside and seeking to rouse the peasants with their speeches. The peasants did not understand, and the police arrested the young revolutionaries. Some were sentenced to prison, and hundreds were deported to remote provinces or to Siberia. It became clear that no progress could be expected from overt action: conspiratorial action was the only hope. In

1876 a new party was founded that took the title of Zemlya i Volya ("Land and Freedom"). Some of its members favoured assassination of prominent officials in reprisal for the maltreatment of their comrades and also as a means to pressure the government in order to extract Western-type political liberties. Experience also had shown them that, while the peasants were physically too scattered to be an effective force and were in any case too apathetic, the workers in the new industrial cities offered a more promising audience. This faction was opposed by others in the party who deprecated assassination, continued to pay more attention to peasants than to workers, and were indifferent to the attainment of political liberties. In 1879 the party split. The politically minded and terrorist wing took the name Narodnaya Volya ("People's Will") and made its aim the assassination of Alexander II. After several unsuccessful attempts, it achieved its aim on March 1 (March 13, New Style), 1881, when the tsar was fatally wounded by a bomb while driving through the capital. All the main leaders of the group were caught by the police, and five of them were hanged.

Shortly before his death the tsar had been considering reforms that would have introduced a few elected representatives into the apparatus of government. His successor, Alexander III (reigned 1881–94), considered these plans. Under the influence of his former tutor, Konstantin Pobedonostsev, the procurator of the Holy Synod (the governing body of the Russian Orthodox Church), he decided to reject them and to reaffirm the principle of autocracy without change. In 1882 he appointed Dmitry Tolstoy minister of the interior. Tolstoy and Pobedonostsev were the moving spirits of the deliberately reactionary policies that followed. Education was further restricted, the work of the zemstvos was hampered, and the village communes were

AS DEPICTED IN AN 1886 PAINTING BY ILYA YEFIMOVICH REPIN, ALEXANDER III RECEIVES THE RURAL DISTRICT ELDERS IN THE YARD OF PETROVSKY PALACE IN MOSCOW. ALEXANDER III PLACED THE SELF-GOVERNING PEASANT COMMUNES UNDER THE SUPERVISION OF LANDED PROPRIETORS APPOINTED BY THE GOVERNMENT.

brought under closer control in 1889 by the institution of the "land commandant" (*zemsky nachalnik*)—an official appointed by the Ministry of the Interior, usually a former officer or a local landowner, who interfered in all aspects of peasant affairs. The office of elected justice of the peace was abolished, and the government was authorized to assume emergency powers when public order was said to be in danger. By this time Russian public officials were better paid and educated, and less addicted to crude corruption, than they had been in the reign of Nicholas I, but they retained their arrogant contempt for the public and especially for the poorer classes. The discriminatory laws against Jews and members of dissenting Christian sects remained a source of widespread injustice, hardship, and resentment.

The repressive policies of Dmitry Tolstoy worked for a time. But the economic development of the following decades created new social tensions and brought into existence new social groups, from whom active opposition once more developed. The zemstvos were in growing conflict with the central authorities. Even their efforts at social improvement of a quite nonpolitical type met with obstruction. The Ministry of the Interior, once the centre of Russia's best reformers, now became a stronghold of resistance. In the obscurantist view of its leading officials, only the central government had the right to care for the public welfare, and zemstvo initiatives were undesirable usurpations of power. Better that nothing should be done at all than that it should be done through the wrong channels. This attitude was manifested in 1891, when crop failures led to widespread famine; government obstruction of relief efforts was widely—though often unfairly—blamed for the peasantry's sufferings. The revival of political activity may be dated from this year. It was accelerated by the death of Alexander III in 1894 and the succession of his son Nicholas II (reigned 1894–1917), who commanded less fear or respect but nevertheless at once antagonized the zemstvo liberals by publicly describing their aspirations for reforms as "senseless dreams." In the late 1890s moderate liberalism, aiming at the establishment of a consultative national assembly, was strong among elected zemstvo members, who were largely members of the landowning class. A more radical attitude, combining elements of liberalism and socialism, was to be found in the professional classes of the cities, including many persons employed by the zemstvos as teachers, doctors, engineers, or statisticians. The growth of an industrial working class provided a mass basis for socialist movements, and by the end of the century some interest in politics was beginning to penetrate even to the peasantry, especially in parts of the middle Volga valley.

THE COMMUNE

The commune, also called mir, was a self-governing community of peasant households that elected its own officials and controlled local forests, fisheries, hunting grounds, and vacant lands. To make taxes imposed on its members more equitable, the mir assumed communal control of the community's arable land and periodically redistributed it among the households, according to their sizes (from 1720).

After serfdom was abolished (1861), the mir was retained as a system of communal land tenure and an organ of local administration. It was economically inefficient; but the central government, having made members of the commune collectively responsible for the payment of state taxes and the fulfillment of local obligations, favoured it. The system was also favoured by Slavophiles and political conservatives, who regarded it as a guardian of old national values, as well as by revolutionary Narodniki ("Populists"), who viewed the mir as the germ of a future socialist society. Despite the efforts of Prime Minister Pyotr A. Stolypin, who initiated a series of agricultural reforms encouraging peasants to assume private ownership, the peasantry universally reverted to communal landholding after the 1917 Revolution.

ECONOMIC AND SOCIAL DEVELOPMENT

Liberation from serfdom was a benefit for the peasants that should not be underrated. The decades that followed brought a growth of prosperity and self-reliance to at least a substantial minority. In 1877, when about four-fifths of the land due to be transferred to the former serfs was actually in their possession, this "allotment land" constituted about half of the arable land in 50 provinces of European Russia. A further one-third of the arable land was still owned by the nobility, and the rest belonged to a variety of individual or collective owners. In 1905 substantially more than half the arable land was in allotment land, while another 10 percent belonged to individual peasants or to peasant associations; the nobility's share of arable land had fallen to a little more than 20 percent. Peasant land had increased by more than 99 million acres (40 million hectares) between 1877 and 1905, of which more than half had been obtained by purchase from landowners and the remainder by the completion of the transfer of allotment land. Peasant purchases had been assisted by loans from the Peasants' Land Bank, set up by the government in 1882. The Nobles' Land Bank, set up in 1885, made loans to landowners at more favourable rates of interest; it may have retarded, but did not prevent, the passage of land from landowners to peasants. In 1894 the rate of interest charged by the two banks was equalized.

Though many peasants improved their position, agriculture remained underdeveloped, and widespread poverty continued to exist. One of the main reasons for this was the indifference of the government to agriculture. The government's economic policy was motivated by the desire for national and military power. This required the growth of industry, and great efforts were made to encourage it. Agriculture was regarded mainly as a source of revenue to pay for industry and the armed forces. Exports of grain made possible imports of raw materials, and taxes paid by peasants filled the state's coffers. The redemption payments were a heavy charge on the peasants' resources, though a gradual fall in the value of money appreciably reduced that burden with the passage of years. Consumption taxes, especially on sugar, tobacco, matches, and oil, affected the peasants, and so did import duties. In 1894 the government introduced a liquor monopoly that drew enormous revenues from the peasants, to whom vodka was a principal solace in a hard life. The techniques and tools of agriculture remained extremely primitive, and farm output low; virtually nothing was done to instruct peasants in modern methods.

The second main cause of peasant poverty was overpopulation. The vast landmass of Russia was, of course, sparsely populated, but the number of persons employed in agriculture per unit of arable land, and relative to output, was extremely high compared with western Europe. There was a vast and increasing surplus of labour in the Russian villages. Outlets were available in seasonal migration to the southern provinces, where labour was needed on the great estates that produced much of the grain that Russia exported. Peasants could also move permanently to new land in Siberia, which at the end of the century was absorbing a yearly influx of 200,000, or they could find seasonal work in the cities or seek permanent employment in the growing industrial sector. These alternatives were not enough to absorb the growing labour surplus, which was most acute in the southern part of central Russia and in northern Ukraine, in the provinces of Kursk and

Poltava. Peasants competed with each other to lease land from the landlords' estates, and this drove rents up. The existence of the large estates came to be resented more and more, and class feeling began to take the form of political demands for further redistribution of land.

The difficulties of agriculture were also increased by the inefficiency of the peasant commune, which had the power to redistribute holdings according to the needs of families and to dictate the rotation of crops to all members. In doing so, it tended to hamper enterprising farmers and protect the incompetent. In defense of the commune it was argued that it ensured a living for everyone and stood for values of solidarity and cooperation that were more important than mere profit and loss. Russian officials also found it useful as a means of collecting taxes and keeping the peasants in order. The 1861 settlement did provide a procedure by which peasants could leave the commune, but it was very complicated and was little used. In practice, the communal system predominated in northern and central Russia, and individual peasant ownership was widespread in Ukraine and in the Polish borderlands. In 1898 in 50 provinces of European Russia, about 198 million acres (80 million hectares) of land were under communal tenure, and about 54 million (22 million) were under individual tenure.

The dispute over the peasant commune divided the ranks both of officialdom and of the government's revolutionary enemies. The Ministry of the Interior, which stood for paternalism and public security at all costs, favoured the commune in the belief that it was a bulwark of conservatism, of traditional Russian social values, and of loyalty to the tsar. The Socialist Revolutionaries favoured it because they took the view that the commune was, at least potentially, the natural unit of a future socialist republic. The Ministry of Finance, concerned with developing capitalism in town and country, objected to the commune as an obstacle to economic progress; it hoped to see a prosperous minority of individual farmers as a basis of a new and more modern type of Russian conservatism. The Social Democrats agreed that the commune must and should be replaced by capitalist ownership, but they saw this only as the next stage in the progress toward a socialist revolution led by urban workers.

The emancipation of the serfs undoubtedly helped capitalist development, though this began rather slowly. A rapid growth of railways came in the 1870s, and in the same decade the exploitation of petroleum began at Baku in Azerbaijan. There was also progress in the textile and sugar industries. Only in the 1890s did the demand for iron and steel, created by the railway program and by military needs in general, begin to be satisfied on a large scale within Russia. By the end of the century there was a massive metallurgical industry in Ukraine, based on the iron ore of Krivoy Rog and the coal of the Donets Basin. The iron industry of the Urals, which lost a large part of its labour force when the serfs became free to leave, lagged far behind. Poland was also an important metallurgical centre. Textiles were concentrated in the central provinces of Moscow and Vladimir; by the end of the century they were drawing much of their raw cotton from the newly conquered lands of Central Asia. Baku was also booming, especially as a supplier of petroleum to the Moscow region. St. Petersburg had begun to develop important engineering and electrical industries. Count Sergey Witte, minister of finance from 1892 to 1903, was able to put Russia on the gold standard in 1897 and to encourage foreign investors. French and Belgian capital was invested mainly in the southern metallurgical industry, British in petroleum, and German in electricity.

Industrial growth began to produce an urban working class, which seemed fated to repeat the history of workers in the early stages of industrial capitalism in Western countries. The workers were unskilled, badly paid, overworked, and miserably housed. Uprooted from the village communities in which they had at least had a recognized place, the peasants' children who flocked into the new industrial agglomerations suffered both physical and moral privation. This was especially true of central Russia, where

RUSSIAN LABOURERS PERFORM JOBS AT A WORKHOUSE IN NIZHNY NOVGOROD IN RUSSIA DURING THE 1890S. MANY URBAN DWELLERS FOUND THE MEAGRE WAGES CHALLENGING TO LIVE ON DURING THESE LEAN TIMES.

the surplus of labour kept wages down to the minimum. It was in St. Petersburg, where employers found it less easy to recruit workers, that the transformation of the amorphous mass of urban poor into a modern working class made the most progress. St. Petersburg employers were also less hostile to government legislation on behalf of the workers. In 1882 Finance Minister Nikolay Khristyanovich Bunge introduced an inspectorate of labour conditions and limited hours of work for children. In 1897 Witte introduced a maximum working day of 11.5 hours for all workers, male or female, and of 10 hours for those engaged in night work. Trade unions were not permitted, though several attempts were made to organize them illegally. The Ministry of the Interior, being more interested in public order than in businessmen's profits, occasionally showed some concern for the workers. In 1901 the head of the Moscow branch of the security police, Colonel Sergey Vasilyevich Zubatov, encouraged the formation of a workers' society intended to rally the workers behind the autocracy, but it was largely infiltrated by Social Democrats. Strikes were strictly forbidden but occurred anyway, especially in 1885, 1896, 1902, and 1903.

A Russian business class also developed rapidly under the umbrella of government policy, benefiting especially from the high protective tariffs and the very high prices paid for government purchases from the metallurgical industry. Russia's industrial progress took place under private capitalism, but it differed from classical Western capitalism in that the motivation of Russian industrial growth was political and military, and the driving force was government policy. Russian and foreign capitalists provided the resources and the organizing skill, and they were richly rewarded. The richness of their rewards accounted for a second difference from classical capitalism: Russian capitalists were completely satisfied with the political system as it was. Whereas English and French capitalists had material and ideological reasons to fight against absolute monarchs and aristocratic upper classes, Russian businessmen accepted the principle and the practice of autocracy.

EDUCATION AND IDEAS

In 1897, at the time of the first modern census in Russia, there were 104,000 persons who had attended or were attending a university—less than 0.1 percent of the population—and 73 percent of these were children of nobles or officials. The number who had studied or were studying in any sort of secondary school was 1,072,977, or less than 1 percent of the population, and 40 percent of these were children of nobles and officials. In 1904, primary schools managed by the Ministry of Education had rather more than 3,000,000 pupils, and those managed by the Orthodox church not quite 2,000,000. The combined figure represented only 27 percent of the children of school age in the empire at that time. Persistent neglect of education could no longer be explained by sheer backwardness and lack of funds: the Russian Empire of 1900 could have afforded a modern school system, albeit rudimentary, if its rulers had considered it a top priority.

In the last half of the 19th century, the word "intelligentsia" came into use in Russia. This word is not precisely definable, for it described both a social group and a state of mind. Essentially, the intelligentsia consisted of persons with a good modern education and a passionate preoccupation with general political and social ideas. Its nucleus was to be found in the liberal professions of law, medicine, teaching, and engineering, which grew in numbers and social prestige as the economy became more complex; yet it also included individuals from outside those professions—private landowners, bureaucrats, and even army officers. The intelligentsia was by its very nature opposed to the existing political and social system, and this opposition coloured its attitude toward culture in general. In particular, the value of works of literature was judged by the intelligentsia according to whether they furthered the cause of social progress. This tradition of social utilitarianism was initiated by the critic Vissarion Belinsky and carried further by Nikolay Aleksandrovich Dobrolyubov in the late 1850s. Its most extreme exponent was Dmitry I. Pisarev, who held that all art is useless and that the only aim of thinking people should be "to solve forever the unavoidable question of hungry and naked people." In the last decades of the century the chief spokesman of social utilitarianism was the sociological writer Nikolay K. Mikhaylovsky, a former supporter of the revolutionary organization Narodnaya Volya. It is hardly an exaggeration to say that Russian literature was faced with two censorships—that of the official servants of the autocracy and that of the social utilitarian radicals. Yet the great writers of this period—Leo Tolstoy, Fyodor Dostoyevsky, and others—though profoundly concerned with social issues, did not conform to these criteria.

The intelligentsia did not consist of active revolutionaries, although it preferred the revolutionaries to the government, but it was from the intelligentsia that the professional revolutionaries were largely recruited. The lack of civil liberties and the prohibition of political parties made it necessary for socialists to use conspiratorial methods. Illegal parties had to have rigid centralized discipline. Yet the emergence of the professional revolutionary, imagined in romantically diabolical terms in the Revolutionary

Catechism of Mikhail Bakunin and Sergey Nechayev in 1869 and sketched more realistically in "What Is to Be Done?" by Vladimir Ilyich Ulyanov, better known as Lenin, in 1902, was not entirely due to the circumstances of the underground political struggle. The revolutionaries were formed also by their sense of mission, by their absolute conviction that they knew best the interests of the masses. For these men and women, revolution was not just a political aim; it was also a substitute for religion. It is worth noting that a proportion of the young revolutionaries of the late 19th century were children of Orthodox priests or persons associated with religious sects. It is also worth noting that the traditional Russian belief in autocracy, the desire for an all-powerful political saviour, and the contempt for legal formalities and processes had left its mark on them. The autocracy of Nicholas II was, of course, odious to them, but this did not mean that autocratic government should be abolished; rather, it should be replaced by the autocracy of the virtuous.

Russian revolutionary socialism at the end of the century was divided into two main streams, each of these being subdivided into a section that favoured conspiratorial tactics and one that aimed at a mass movement to be controlled by its members. The Socialist Revolutionary Party (Socialist Revolutionaries; founded in 1901 from a number of groups more or less derived from Narodnaya Volya) first hoped that Russia could bypass capitalism; when it became clear that this could not be done, they aimed to limit its operation and build a socialist order based on village communes. The land was to be socialized but worked by peasants on the principle of "labour ownership." The Russian Social-Democratic Workers' Party (Social Democrats; founded in 1898 from a number of illegal working-class groups) believed that the future lay with industrialization and a socialist order based on the working class. The Socialist Revolutionaries were divided between their extreme terrorist wing, the Fighting Organization, and a broader and looser membership that at one end merged imperceptibly with radical middle-class liberalism. The Social Democrats were divided between Lenin's group, which took the name Bolshevik (derived from the Russian word for "majority," after a majority won by his group at one particular vote during the second congress of the party, held in Brussels and London in 1903), and a number of other groups that were by no means united but that came to be collectively known as Menshevik (derived from the word for "minority"). The personal, ideological, and programmatic issues involved in their quarrels were extremely complex, but it is a permissible oversimplification to say that Lenin favoured rigid discipline while the Mensheviks aimed at creating a mass labour movement of the western European type, that the Mensheviks were much more willing to cooperate with nonsocialist liberals than were the Bolsheviks, and that Lenin paid much more attention to the peasants as a potential revolutionary force than did the Mensheviks. These divisions arose because the Mensheviks adhered to orthodox Marxism, while Lenin was prepared to rework basic Marxist thought to fit Russian political reality as he saw it.

RUSSIFICATION POLICIES

After the Crimean War the Russian government made some attempt to introduce in Poland a new system acceptable to the Polish population. The leading figure on the Polish side was the nobleman Aleksander Wielopolski. His pro-Russian program proved unacceptable to the Poles. Tension increased, and in January 1863 armed rebellion broke out. This rebellion was put down, being suppressed with special severity in the Lithuanian and Ukrainian borderlands. In order to punish the Polish country gentry for their part in the insurrection, the Russian authorities carried out a land reform on terms exceptionally favourable to the Polish peasants. Its authors were Nikolay Milyutin and Yury Samarin, who genuinely desired to benefit the peasants. The reform was followed, however, by an anti-Polish policy in education and other areas. In the 1880s this went so far that the language of instruction even in primary schools in areas of purely Polish population was Russian. At first, all classes of Poles passively acquiesced in their defeat, while clinging to their language and national consciousness, but in the 1890s two strong, though of course illegal, political parties appeared—the National Democrats and the Polish Socialist Party, both fundamentally anti-Russian.

After 1863 the authorities also severely repressed all signs of Ukrainian nationalist activity. In 1876 all publications in Ukrainian, other than historical documents, were prohibited. In Eastern Galicia, however, which lay just across the Austrian border and had a population of several million Ukrainians, not only the language but also political activity flourished. There the great Ukrainian historian Mikhail Hrushevsky and the socialist writer Mikhail Drahomanov published their works; Ukrainian political literature was smuggled across the border. In the 1890s small illegal groups of Ukrainian democrats and socialists existed on Russian soil.

Starting in the 1860s the government embarked on a policy designed to strengthen the position of the Russian language and nationality in the borderlands of the empire. This policy is often described as Russification. The emphasis on the Russian language could also be seen as an attempt to make governing the empire easier and more efficient. However, though Russian was to be the lingua franca, or common language, the government never explicitly demanded that its non-Russian subjects abandon their own languages, nationalities, or religions. On the other hand, conversions to Orthodoxy were welcomed, and converts were not allowed to revert to their former religions. The government policy of Russification found its parallel in the overtly Russian nationalist tone of several influential newspapers and journals. Nor was Russian society immune to the attraction of national messianism, as the popularity of Nikolay Yakovlevich Danilevsky's article "Russia and Europe" in the decades after its first appearance in 1869 attested. For most supporters of Russification, however, the policy's main aim was to consolidate a Russian national identity and loyalty at the empire's centre and to combat the potential threat of imperial disintegration in the face of minority nationalism.

Ironically, by the late 19th and early 20th century some of the most prominent objects of Russification were peoples who had shown consistent loyalty to the empire and now found themselves confronted by government policies that aimed to curtail the rights and privileges of their culture and nationality. The Germans of the Baltic provinces were deprived of their university, and their ancient secondary schools were Russified. The Latvians and Estonians did not object to action by the government against the Germans, whom they had reason to dislike as landowners and rich burghers, but the prospect of the German language being replaced by the Russian had no attraction for them, and they strongly resented the pressure to abandon their Lutheran faith for Orthodoxy. The attempt to abolish many aspects of Finnish autonomy united the Finns in opposition to St. Petersburg in the 1890s. In 1904 the son of a Finnish senator assassinated the Russian governor-general, and passive resistance to Russian policies was almost universal. Effective and widespread passive resistance also occurred among the traditionally Russophile Armenians of the Caucasus when the Russian authorities began to interfere with the organization of the Armenian church and to close the schools maintained from its funds.

Of the Muslim peoples of the empire, those who suffered most from Russification were the most economically and culturally advanced, the Tatars of the Volga valley. Attempts by the Orthodox church to convert Muslims and the rivalry between Muslims and Orthodox to convert small national groups of Finno-Ugric people who were still pagans caused growing mutual hostility. By the end of the century the Tatars had developed a substantial merchant class and the beginnings of a national intelligentsia. Modern schools, maintained by merchants' funds, were creating a new Tatar educated elite that was increasingly receptive to modern democratic ideas. In Central Asia, on the other hand, modern influences had barely made themselves felt, and there was no Russification. In those newly conquered lands, Russian colonial administration was paternalistic and limited: like the methods of "indirect rule" in the British and French empires, it made no systematic attempt to change old ways.

The position of the Jews was hardest of all. As a result of their history and religious traditions, as well as of centuries of social and economic discrimination, the Jews were overwhelmingly concentrated in commercial and intellectual professions. They were thus prominent both as businessmen and as political radicals, hateful to the bureaucrats as socialists and to the lower classes as capitalists. The pogroms, or anti-Jewish riots, which broke out in various localities in the months after the assassination of Alexander II, effectively ended any dreams for assimilation and "enlightenment" on the western European pattern for Russia's

Jewish community. At this time there also arose the oft-repeated accusation that anti-Semitic excesses were planned and staged by the authorities, not only in Ukraine in 1881 but also in Kishinev in 1903 and throughout the Jewish Pale of Settlement in 1905. The view of government-sponsored pogroms has not, however, been corroborated by documental evidence. Indeed, the officials in St. Petersburg were too concerned with maintaining order to organize pogroms that might pose a direct threat to that order. However, some local government officials were certainly at least remiss in their duties in protecting Jewish lives and properties and at worse in cahoots with the anti-Semitic rioters. The most important result of the 1881 pogrom wave was the promulgation in May 1882 of the notorious "temporary rules," which further restricted Jewish rights and remained in effect to the very end of the Russian Empire. By the turn of the century the terms "Jews" and "revolutionaries" had come to be synonymous for some officials.

FOREIGN POLICY

During the second half of the 19th century, Russian foreign policy gave about equal emphasis to the Balkans and East Asia. The friendship with Germany and Austria weakened, and in the 1890s the Triple Alliance of Germany, Austria-Hungary, and Italy stood face to face with a Dual Alliance of France and Russia.

The demilitarization of the Black Sea coast that had resulted from the Crimean War was ended by the London Conference of 1871, which allowed Russia to rebuild its naval forces. In 1876 the Serbo-Turkish War produced an outburst of Pan-Slav feeling in Russia. Partly under its influence, but mainly in pursuit of traditional strategic aims, Russia declared war on Turkey in April 1877. After overpowering heavy Turkish resistance at the fortress of Pleven in Bulgaria, the Russian forces advanced almost to Istanbul. By the Treaty of San Stefano of March 1878 the Turks accepted the creation of a large independent Bulgarian state. Fearing that this would be a Russian vassal, giving Russia mastery over all the Balkans and the straits, Britain and Austria-Hungary opposed the treaty. At the international Congress of Berlin, held in June 1878, Russia had to accept a much smaller Bulgaria. This was regarded by Russian public opinion as a bitter humiliation, for which the German chancellor Otto von Bismarck was blamed. In 1885–87 a new international crisis was caused by Russian interference in Bulgarian affairs, with Britain and Austria-Hungary again opposing Russia. Once more, Russia suffered a political reverse. In the 1890s, despite the pro-Russian sentiment of many Serbs and Bulgarians, neither country's government was much subject to Russian influence. In the crises that arose in connection with the Turkish Armenians and over Crete and Macedonia, Russian policy was extremely cautious and on the whole tended to support the Turkish government. In 1897 an Austro-Russian agreement was made on spheres of influence in the Balkans.

The attempt of Bismarck to restore Russo-German friendship through the Reinsurance Treaty of 1887, with a view to an ultimate restoration of the alliance of Russia, Germany, and Austria, did not survive Bismarck's fall from power in 1890. The Russian government, alarmed by indications of a closer cooperation between the Triple Alliance and Britain and by some signs of a pro-Polish attitude in Berlin, reluctantly turned toward France. The French needed an ally against both Germany and Britain; the Russians needed French capital, in the form both of loans to the Russian government and of investment in Russian industry. The Franco-Russian alliance was signed in August 1891 and was supplemented by a military convention. Essentially, the alliance was directed against Germany, for it was only in a war with Germany that each could help the other. Later, however, there were to be plans in case war with Britain broke out.

Russia established diplomatic and commercial relations with Japan by three treaties between 1855 and 1858. In 1860, by the Treaty of Beijing, Russia acquired from China a long strip of Pacific coastline south of the mouth of the Amur and began to build the naval base of Vladivostok. In 1867 the Russian government sold Alaska to the United States for $7.2 million. The Treaty of St. Petersburg between Russia and Japan in 1875 gave Russia sole control over all of Sakhalin and gave Japan the Kuril Islands.

The systematic Russian conquest of Turkistan, the region of settled population and ancient culture lying to the south of the Kazakh steppes, began in the 1860s. This was watched with distrust by the British authorities in India, and fear of Russian interference in Afghanistan led to the Anglo-Afghan War of 1878–80. In the 1880s Russian expansion extended to the Turkmen lands on the east coast of the Caspian Sea, whose people offered much stiffer military resistance. The Russian conquest of Merv in 1884 caused alarm in Kolkata (Calcutta), and in March 1885 a clash between Russian and Afghan troops produced a major diplomatic crisis between Britain and Russia. An agreement on frontier delimitation was reached in September 1885, and for the next decades Central Asian affairs did not have a major effect on Anglo-Russian relations. At the same time, Russia and Britain battled for influence over the weakening Iranian state.

Much more serious was the situation in East Asia. In 1894–95 the long-standing rivalry between the Japanese and Chinese in Korea led to a war between the two Asian empires, which the Japanese won decisively. Russia faced the choice of collaborating with Japan (with which relations had been fairly good for some years) at the expense of China or assuming the role of protector of China against Japan. The tsar chose the second policy, largely under the influence of Count Witte. Together with the French and German governments, the Russians

Le Petit Journal

SUPPLÉMENT ILLUSTRÉ

Huit pages : CINQ centimes

SAMEDI 14 MARS 1891

UN AMI DE LA FRANCE

(L'EMPEREUR DE RUSSIE ALEXANDRE III)

THIS FRENCH NEWSPAPER, FROM MARCH 14, 1891, SHOWS ALEXANDER III AS A FRIEND OF FRANCE AFTER HE SIGNED AN ALLIANCE WITH THE COUNTRY.

demanded that the Japanese return to China the Liaodong Peninsula, which they had taken in the treaty of peace. Russia then concluded an alliance with China in 1896, which included the establishment of the Russian-owned Chinese Eastern Railway, which was to cross northern Manchuria from west to east, linking Siberia with Vladivostok, and was to be administered by Russian personnel and a Russian police force with extraterritorial rights. In 1898 the Russian government went still further and acquired from China the same Liaodong Peninsula of which it had deprived the Japanese three years earlier. There the Russians built a naval base in ice-free waters at Port Arthur (Lüshun; now in Dalian, China). They also obtained extraterritorial rights of ownership and management of a southern Manchurian railroad that was to stretch from north to south, linking Port Arthur with the Chinese Eastern Railway at the junction of Harbin. When in 1900 the European powers sent armed forces to relieve their diplomatic missions in Beijing, besieged by the Boxer Rebellion, the Russian government used this as an opportunity to bring substantial military units into Manchuria. All of this bitterly antagonized the Japanese. They might have been willing, nonetheless, to write off Manchuria as a Russian sphere of influence provided that Russia recognize Japanese priority in Korea, but the Russian government would not do this. It was not so much that the tsar himself wished to dominate all of East Asia; it was rather that he was beset by advisers with several rival schemes and could not bring himself to reject any of them, particularly since he underestimated Japan's resolution and power. The British government, fearing that Russia would be able to establish domination over the Chinese government and so interfere with the interests of Britain in other parts of China, made an alliance with Japan in January 1902. Negotiations between Russia and Japan continued, but they were insincere on both sides. On the night of January 26/27 (February 8/9, New Style), 1904, Japanese forces made a surprise attack on Russian warships in Port Arthur, and the Russo-Japanese War began.

CHAPTER 2

THE BACKDROP OF REVOLUTION AND THE LAST YEARS OF TSARDOM

Japan successfully ended a war against China in 1895. This was followed, however, by demands from Russia, Germany, and France that Japan evacuate Port Arthur (now Lüshun) and the Liaodong Peninsula, on which Port Arthur was located. The entire peninsula had earlier been ceded to Japan by China. Japan yielded, but in 1898 Russia seized the peninsula for itself. Later Russia occupied all of Manchuria. Japan pressed Russia to withdraw, but Russia refused. A Russian concession for timber cutting in the Yalu River valley, which lies between China and Korea, was also protested by the Japanese, who viewed the concession as an attempt by the Russians to bring Korea under Russian control.

THE RUSSO-JAPANESE WAR

Japan prepared for war by strengthening its army and navy. It also entered into an alliance with Great Britain in 1902. The British were wary of Russian domination of East Asia. In February 1904 Japan broke diplomatic relations with Russia and launched a surprise torpedo attack on the Russian fleet at Port Arthur. Japanese armies invaded the peninsula and dealt the Russians a series of defeats. The chief land battles were at

UN BEAU TRAIT D'AUDACE
Estafettes russes forçant le passage vers Port-Arthur

HERE, THE RUSSIAN CAVALRY LAUNCHES A SURPRISE ATTACK ON THE JAPANESE ON THE ROAD TO PORT ARTHUR IN MANCHURIA IN 1904 DURING THE RUSSO-JAPANESE WAR. AFTER THE RUSSIANS SURRENDERED IN JANUARY 1905, THEY HAD TO GIVE UP CONTROL OF KOREA AND MUCH OF MANCHURIA TO JAPAN.

Liaoyang in 1904 and at Mukden (now Shenyang) in 1905. The Russian ships were either destroyed or were penned up in Port Arthur. Russia's Baltic fleet, after a cruise around the Cape of Good Hope, was defeated in Tsushima Strait in the battle of the Sea of Japan.

Russia fought under many handicaps. Its source of men and supplies was thousands of miles from the scene of battle. The only connecting link was the inadequate single-track Trans-Siberian Railroad. When internal revolt shook Russia in 1905, the nation sued for peace. President Theodore Roosevelt of the United States served as mediator at a peace conference in Portsmouth, New Hampshire. The resulting Treaty of Portsmouth (September 5, 1905) gave Russia's rights in Port Arthur and the Liaodong Peninsula to Japan. It also gave Japan the southern half of the island of Sakhalin. In addition, Russia agreed to evacuate Manchuria and to recognize Japan's interests in Korea.

THE TRANS-SIBERIAN RAILROAD

Siberia is a vast expanse of land that stretches across Russia from the Ural Mountains in the west to the Pacific Ocean in the east. In the 19th century Siberia was Russia's frontier—thinly populated, largely unexplored, yet possessing vast economic potential. Settlement in the region remained sparse until the building of the Trans-Siberian Railroad, which made large-scale immigration possible. Within Siberia a number of today's larger cities—such as Novosibirsk and Yekaterinburg—owe their development to the completion of the railroad.

(continued on the next page)

(continued from the previous page)

Building the railroad was a great feat of engineering because of the very difficult terrain and extremes of temperature—Siberia can be one of the coldest places in the world. The Siberian section of the line, running from Chelyabinsk in the west to Vladivostok on the Pacific, is about 4,400 miles (7,000 kilometers) long. If the line connecting St. Petersburg to Moscow is added, the whole length is about 5,900 miles (9,500 kilometers)—the longest single line of track in the world.

Construction of the Trans-Siberian Railroad began in 1891. Work started at the same time from both the eastern and western terminals. The plan originally called for an all-Russian road, but a treaty with China in 1896 enabled the Russians to construct an 800-mile (1,300-kilometer) line through Manchuria, thus shortening the distance to Vladivostok. After Manchuria passed to Japanese hands following the Russo-Japanese War of 1904–05, the Russians proceeded with a longer railway entirely on their own territory.

One of the main obstacles to completion of the line was Lake Baikal, where there was a ferry service. A loop around the lakeshore was completed in 1905. By 1916 the Amur River line north of the Chinese border was finished, and there was a continuous railway on Russian land from Moscow across Siberia.

BLOODY SUNDAY

The Russian defeat in the Russo-Japanese War finally brought to a head a variety of political discontents simmering back at home. First the professional strata, especially in the zemstvos and municipalities, organized a banquet campaign in favour of a popularly elected legislative assembly. Then, on January 9 (January 22, New Style), 1905, the priest Georgy Gapon (leader of the Assembly of Russian Factory Workers) arranged a mass demonstration of St. Petersburg workers, hoping to present the workers' request for reforms directly to the emperor. Having told the authorities of his plan, he led the workers—who were peacefully carrying religious icons, pictures of Nicholas, and petitions citing their grievances and desired reforms—toward the square before the Winter Palace. Nicholas was not in the city. The chief of the security police—Nicholas's uncle, Grand Duke Vladimir—tried to stop the march and then ordered his police to fire upon the demonstrators. More than 100 marchers were killed, and several hundred were wounded.

WHEN NICHOLAS II'S TROOPS FIRED ON DEMONSTRATORS IN FRONT OF THE WINTER PALACE IN ST. PETERSBURG ON JANUARY 9, 1905 (JANUARY 22, NEW STYLE), THE MASSACRE BECAME KNOWN AS BLOODY SUNDAY.

News of this massacre, known as Bloody Sunday, spread quickly, and very soon most of the other social classes and ethnic groups in the empire were in an uproar. There were student demonstrations, workers' strikes, peasant insurrections, and mutinies in both the army and navy. The peasants organized themselves through their traditional village assembly, the mir, to decide when and how to seize the land or property of the landlords. The workers, on the other hand, created new institutions, the Soviets of Workers' Deputies: these, consisting of elected delegates from the factories and workshops of a whole town, organized the strike movement there, negotiated with the employers and police, and sometimes kept up basic municipal services during the crisis.

THE OCTOBER MANIFESTO

The October Manifesto (Oct. 30 [Oct. 17, Old Style], 1905) was the document issued by Nicholas II that in effect marked the end of unlimited autocracy in Russia and ushered in an era of constitutional monarchy. Threatened by the events of the Russian Revolution of 1905, Nicholas faced the choice of establishing a military dictatorship or granting a constitution. Although both the tsar and his advising minister Sergey Yulyevich, Count Witte, had reservations about the latter option, it was determined to be tactically the better choice. Nicholas thus issued the October Manifesto, which promised to guarantee civil liberties (e.g., freedom of speech, press, and assembly), to establish a broad franchise, and to create a legislative body (the Duma) whose members would be popularly elected and whose approval would be necessary before the enactment of any legislation.

The manifesto satisfied enough of the moderate participants in the revolution to weaken the forces against the government and allow the revolution to be crushed. Only then did the government formally fulfill

ILYA YEFIMOVICH REPIN'S PAINTING THE DEMONSTRATION OF OCTOBER 17, 1905 DEPICTS JUBILANT MARCHERS AFTER NICHOLAS II ISSUED THE OCTOBER MANIFESTO. THE OCTOBER MANIFESTO PROMISED TO GUARANTEE FREEDOM OF SPEECH, PRESS, AND ASSEMBLY, ESTABLISH BROAD FRANCHISE, AND CREATE A LEGISLATIVE BODY CALLED THE DUMA.

the promises of the manifesto. On April 23, 1906, the Fundamental Laws, which were to serve as a constitution, were promulgated. The Duma that was created had two houses rather than one, however, and members of only one of them were to be popularly elected. Further, the Duma had only limited control over the budget and none at all over the executive branch of the government. In addition, the civil rights and suffrage rights granted by the Fundamental Laws were far more limited than those promised by the manifesto.

THE RUSSIAN REVOLUTION OF 1905

The revolutionary movement reached its climax in October 1905, with the declaration of a general strike and the formation of a soviet (council) in St. Petersburg itself. Most cities, including the capital, were paralyzed, and Sergey Yulyevich, Count Witte, who had just concluded peace negotiations with the Japanese, recommended that the government yield to the demands of the liberals and create an elected legislative assembly. This the tsar reluctantly consented to do, in the manifesto of October 17 (October 30, New Style), 1905. It did not end the unrest, however. In a number of towns, armed bands of monarchists, known as Black Hundreds, organized pogroms against Jewish quarters and also attacked students and known left-wing activists. In Moscow the soviet unleashed an armed insurrection in December, which had to be put down with artillery, resulting in considerable loss of life. Peasant unrest and mutinies in the armed services continued well into 1906 and even 1907.

Throughout the period from 1905 to 1907, disorders were especially violent in non-Russian regions of the empire, where the revolutionary movement took on an added ethnic dimension, as in Poland, the Baltic provinces, Georgia, and parts of Ukraine. There was also persistent fighting between Armenians and Azerbaijanis in the towns of Transcaucasia.

A campaign of terrorism, waged by the Maximalists of the Socialist Revolutionary Party against policemen and officials, claimed hundreds of lives in 1905–07. The police felt able to combat it only by infiltrating their agents into the revolutionary parties and particularly into the terrorist detachments of these parties. This use of double agents (or agents provocateurs, as they were often known) did much to demoralize both the revolutionaries and the police and to undermine the reputation of both with the public at large. The nadir was reached in 1908, when it was disclosed that Yevno Azef, longtime head of the terrorist wing of the Socialist Revolutionary Party, was also an employee of the department of police and had for years been both betraying his revolutionary colleagues and organizing the murders of his official superiors.

The split in the Social Democratic Party was deepened by the failure of the 1905 revolution. Both Mensheviks and Bolsheviks agreed that a further revolution would be needed but disagreed fundamentally on the way to bring it about. The Mensheviks favoured cooperation with the bourgeois parties in the Duma, the new legislative assembly, in order to legislate civil rights and then use them to organize the workers for the next stage of the class struggle. The Bolsheviks regarded the Duma purely as a propaganda forum, and Lenin drew from 1905 the lesson that in Russia, where the bourgeoisie was weak, the revolutionaries could combine the bourgeois and proletarian stages of the revolution by organizing the peasantry as allies of the workers. He was also moving closer to Leon Trotsky's theory that the forthcoming Russian revolution, taking place in the country that was the "weak link" of international imperialism, would spark a world revolution. Lenin did not reveal the full extent of the changes in his ideas until 1917, but in 1912 the split with the Mensheviks was finalized when the Bolsheviks called their own congress in Prague that year, claiming to speak in the name of the entire Social Democratic Party.

THE STATE DUMA

The October Manifesto had split the opposition. The professional strata, now reorganizing themselves in liberal parties, basically accepted it and set about trying to make the new legislature, the State Duma, work in the interest of reform. The two principal Socialist parties, the Socialist Revolutionaries and the Social Democrats, saw the manifesto as just a first step and the Duma (which at first they boycotted) as merely a tribune to be exploited to project their revolutionary ideas.

The empire's Fundamental Laws were amended in 1906 to take account of the Duma. Russia was still described as an autocracy, though the adjective "unlimited" was no longer attached to the term, and an article confirming that no law could take effect without the consent of the Duma effectively annulled its meaning. Alongside the Duma there was to be an upper chamber, the State Council, half of its members appointed by the emperor and half elected by established institutions such as the zemstvos and municipalities, business organizations, the Academy of Sciences, and so on. Both chambers had budgetary rights, the right to veto any law, and the ability to initiate legislation. On the other hand, the government was to be appointed, as before, by the emperor, who in practice seldom chose members of the Duma or State Council to be ministers. In addition, the emperor had the right to dissolve the legislative chambers at any time and, under Article 87, to pass emergency decrees when they were not in session.

The Duma electoral law, though complicated, did give the franchise to most adult males. The first elections, held in spring 1906, produced a relative majority for the Constitutional Democratic Party (Kadets), a radical liberal group drawn largely from the professional strata that wished to go beyond the October Manifesto to a full constitutional monarchy on the British model and to grant autonomy to the non-Russian nationalities. The next largest caucus, the Labour Group (Trudoviki), included a large number of peasants and some socialists who had ignored their comrades' boycott. The two parties demanded amnesty for political prisoners, equal rights for Jews, autonomy for Poland, and—most important of all—expropriation of landed estates for the peasants. These demands were totally unacceptable to the government, which used its powers to dissolve the Duma. The new premier, Pyotr Arkadyevich Stolypin, then used Article 87 to pass his own agrarian reform, known as the Stolypin land reform, and to institute special summary courts-martial against terrorists; under the jurisdiction of these courts, some 600–1,000 suspects were executed.

In early 1907 new elections were held; to the government's disappointment, the Social Democrats, having abandoned their boycott, did very well, coming in as the third-largest party, behind the Kadets and the Trudoviki. The monarchists also performed better than before, so that the house was sharply polarized, but with a preponderance on the left. Unable to pass his agrarian law through it or to cooperate with its majority in any other way, Stolypin advised the tsar to dissolve the Second Duma on June 3 (June 16, New Style), 1907.

Nicholas did not, however, abolish the Duma altogether, as some of his advisers wished. Instead, he and Stolypin altered the electoral law in favour of landowners, wealthier townsfolk, and Russians to the detriment of peasants, workers, and non-Russians. The Third Duma, elected in autumn 1907, and the Fourth, elected in autumn 1912, were therefore more congenial to the government. The leading caucus in both Dumas was the Union of October 17 (known as the Octobrists), whose strength was among the landowners of the Russian heartland. The Octobrists acknowledged the October Manifesto as a sufficient basis for cooperation with the government and accepted Stolypin's agrarian program as well as his desire to strengthen the position of the Russian nation throughout the empire.

In practice, however, their cooperation did not bear much legislative fruit beyond the agrarian reform. Many nobles were worried by Stolypin's proposed reform of local government and justice, which would have weakened their dominant position in the localities. They were also alarmed that more and more land was passing from their control to other social classes. Their opposition was articulated by a pressure group known as the United Nobility, which had numerous members in the State Council and close personal links with the imperial court. Stolypin increasingly found that his reform measures, passed by the Duma, were being blocked in the State Council.

Frustrated but not wanting to lose all momentum, Stolypin fell back on nationalist measures, for which he could rely on support from his right-wing opponents both in the Duma and the State Council. Such was the bill restricting Finland's special liberties, passed in 1910. He proposed introducing zemstvos into the western provinces; since most landowners there were Polish, he added a special provision to bolster the vote of Russian peasants. The right wing of the State Council objected to this weakening of the landowners, and, receiving the tacit support of the emperor, they defeated the vital clause in the bill in March 1911. Stolypin, dismayed and angry, suspended both houses for three days and introduced the western zemstvos under Article 87. This egregious violation of the spirit of the Fundamental Laws lost him the support of the Octobrists, who went into opposition. Stolypin was, then, already fatally weakened politically when he was assassinated in September 1911. His murderer was both a Socialist Revolutionary and a police agent whose motives have remained obscure.

Although the legislative achievements of the Duma were meagre, it should not be written off as an ineffective body. It voted credits for a planned expansion of education that was on target to introduce compulsory primary schooling by 1922. Although it could not create or bring down governments, it could exert real pressure on ministers, especially during the budget debates in which even foreign and military affairs (constitutionally the preserve of the emperor alone) came under the deputies' scrutiny. These debates were extensively reported in the newspapers, where they could not be censored, and enormously intensified public awareness of political issues. Partly as a result, the period 1905–14 saw a huge growth in the publication of newspapers, periodicals, and books, both in the capital cities and in the provinces.

Not all the results of this heightened political awareness were happy for the government, of course. In 1910–11, following the death of Leo Tolstoy, who had been excommunicated by the Orthodox church and was refused an ecclesiastical burial, there was serious student unrest, and several Moscow State University professors resigned in protest at government arbitrariness. Furthermore, in 1912, after a disorder at the Lena gold mines, where some 200 workers were killed by troops, the workers' movement revived. Strikes and demonstrations broke out in many of the largest cities, culminating in the erection of barricades in St. Petersburg in July 1914. This time, however, the workers were on their own: there was no sign that peasants, students, or professional people were prepared to join their struggle.

In this Russian caricature, the monk Grigory Yefimovich Rasputin is shown manipulating Tsar Nicholas II and Tsarina Alexandra as puppets.

One area where the failure to reform had very serious effects was in the church. Most prelates and clergymen wanted to see the Orthodox church given greater independence in relation to the state, perhaps by restoring the patriarchate and assigning authority within the church to a synod elected by clergy and laity. Many also favoured internal reform by strengthening the parish, ending the split between white (parish) and black (monastic) clergy, and bringing liturgy and scriptures closer to the people. An elected church council was to have taken place in 1906 to debate these reforms, but in the end Stolypin and Nicholas decided not to convene it, as they feared its deliberations would intensify political discontent in the country. Thus, the church remained under secular domination until 1917 and fell increasingly under the influence of Grigory Yefimovich Rasputin, a starets (holy man) of dubious reputation who became a favourite of the imperial couple because he was able to stanch the bleeding of their son Alexis, who suffered from hemophilia.

NICHOLAS II AND ALEXANDRA

Nikolay Aleksandrovich, later called Nicholas II, was born on May 6 (May 18, New Style), 1868, in Tsarskoye Selo (now Pushkin), near St. Petersburg, Russia. He was the eldest son and heir apparent (tsesarevich) of the tsarevich Aleksandr Aleksandrovich (emperor as Alexander III from 1881) and his consort Maria Fyodorovna (Dagmar of Denmark).

Neither by upbringing nor by temperament was Nicholas fitted for the complex tasks that awaited him as autocratic ruler of a vast empire. He had received a military education from his tutor, and his tastes and interests were those of the average young Russian officers of his day.

(continued on the next page)

Nicholas II and Alexandra are photographed here around 1906–07 with their children, Grand Duchesses Olga, Tatiana, Maria, and Anastasia, and Tsarevich Alexis.

(continued from the previous page)

He had few intellectual pretensions but delighted in physical exercise and the trappings of army life: uniforms, insignia, and parades. Yet on formal occasions he felt ill at ease. Though he possessed great personal charm, he was by nature timid; he shunned close contact with his subjects, preferring the privacy of his family circle. His domestic life was serene. To his wife, Alexandra, whom he had married on November 26, 1894, Nicholas was passionately devoted. A granddaughter of Queen Victoria and daughter of Louis IV, Grand Duke of Hesse-Darmstadt, Alexandra came to dominate Nicholas. Succeeding his father on November 1, 1894, Nicholas was crowned tsar in Moscow on May 26, 1896.

Alexandra proved to be unpopular at court and turned to mysticism for solace. She had the strength of character that Nicholas lacked, and Nicholas fell completely under her sway. Through her near-fanatical acceptance of Orthodoxy and her belief in autocratic rule, she felt it her sacred duty to help reassert Nicholas's absolute power, which had been limited by reforms in 1905. In 1904 the tsarevich Alexis was born; she had previously given birth to four daughters (Olga, Tatiana, Maria, and Anastasia). The tsarevich suffered from hemophilia, and Alexandra's overwhelming concern for his life led her to seek the aid of a debauched "holy man" who possessed hypnotic powers, Grigory Yefimovich Rasputin. Rasputin had an obviously beneficial effect on Alexis. Alexandra came to venerate Rasputin as a saint sent by God to save the throne and as a voice of the common people, who, she believed, remained loyal to the emperor. Under her influence Nicholas sought the advice of spiritualists and faith healers, most notably Rasputin, who acquired great power over the imperial couple.

Nicholas also had other irresponsible favourites, often men of dubious probity who provided him with a distorted picture of Russian life, but one that he found more comforting than that contained in official reports. He distrusted his ministers, mainly because he felt them to be intellectually superior to himself and feared they sought to usurp his sovereign prerogatives. His view of his role as autocrat was childishly simple: he derived his authority from God, to whom alone he was responsible, and it was his sacred duty to preserve his absolute power intact. He lacked, however, the strength of will necessary in one who had such an exalted conception of his task. In pursuing the path of duty, Nicholas had to wage a continual struggle against himself, suppressing his natural indecisiveness and assuming a mask of self-confident resolution. His dedication to the dogma of autocracy was an inadequate substitute for a constructive policy, which alone could have prolonged the imperial regime.

(continued on the next page)

THE RUSSIAN REVOLUTION
THE FALL OF THE TSARS AND THE RISE OF COMMUNISM

(continued from the previous page)

Soon after his accession Nicholas proclaimed his uncompromising views in an address to liberal deputies from the zemstvos, the self-governing local assemblies, in which he dismissed as "senseless dreams" their aspirations to share in the work of government. He met the rising groundswell of popular unrest with intensified police repression. In foreign policy, his naïveté and lighthearted attitude toward international obligations sometimes embarrassed his professional diplomats; for example, he concluded an alliance with the German emperor William II during their meeting at Björkö in July 1905, although Russia was already allied with France, Germany's traditional enemy.

Nicholas was the first Russian sovereign to show personal interest in Asia, visiting in 1891, while still tsesarevich, India, China, and Japan; later he nominally supervised the construction of the Trans-Siberian Railway. His attempt to maintain and strengthen Russian influence in Korea, where Japan also had a foothold, was partly responsible for the Russo-Japanese War (1904–05). Russia's defeat not only frustrated Nicholas's grandiose dreams of making Russia a great Eurasian power, with China, Tibet, and Persia under its control, but also presented him with serious problems at home, where discontent grew into the revolutionary movement of 1905.

Nicholas considered all who opposed him, regardless of their views, as malicious conspirators. Disregarding the advice of his future prime minister Sergey Yulyevich Witte, he refused to make concessions to the constitutionalists until events forced him to yield more than might have been necessary had he been more flexible. On March 3, 1905, he reluctantly agreed to create a national representative assembly, or Duma, with consultative powers, and by the manifesto of October 30 he promised a constitutional regime under which no law was to take effect without the Duma's consent, as well as a democratic franchise and civil liberties. Nicholas, however, cared little for keeping promises extracted from him under duress. He strove to regain his former powers and ensured that in the new

52

Fundamental Laws (May 1906) he was still designated an autocrat. He furthermore patronized an extremist right-wing organization, the Union of the Russian People, which sanctioned terrorist methods and disseminated anti-Semitic propaganda. Witte, whom he blamed for the October Manifesto, was soon dismissed, and the first two Dumas were prematurely dissolved as "insubordinate."

Pyotr Arkadyevich Stolypin, who replaced Witte and carried out the coup of June 16, 1907, dissolving the second Duma, was loyal to the dynasty and a capable statesman. But the emperor distrusted him and allowed his position to be undermined by intrigue. Stolypin was one of those who dared to speak out about Rasputin's influence and thereby incurred the displeasure of the empress. In such cases Nicholas generally hesitated but ultimately yielded to Alexandra's pressure. To prevent exposure of the scandalous hold Rasputin had on the imperial family, Nicholas interfered arbitrarily in matters properly within the competence of the Holy Synod, backing reactionary elements against those concerned about the Orthodox church's prestige.

After its ambitions in the Far East were checked by Japan, Russia turned its attention to the Balkans. Nicholas sympathized with the national aspirations of the Slavs and was anxious to win control of the Turkish straits but tempered his expansionist inclinations with a sincere desire to preserve peace among the Great Powers. After the assassination of the Austrian archduke Francis Ferdinand at Sarajevo, he tried hard to avert the impending war by diplomatic action and resisted, until July 30, 1914, the pressure of the military for general, rather than partial, mobilization.

The outbreak of World War I temporarily strengthened the monarchy, but Nicholas did little to maintain his people's confidence. The Duma was slighted, and voluntary patriotic organizations were hampered in their efforts; the gulf between the ruling group and public opinion grew steadily wider.

Nicholas II did not, in fact, interfere unduly in operational decisions, but his departure for headquarters had serious political

(continued on the next page)

(continued from the previous page)

consequences. After Nicholas left for the front in August 1915, in his absence, supreme power in effect passed, with his approval and encouragement, to the empress. Rasputin's influence was a public scandal, but Alexandra silenced all criticism. Alexandra turned Nicholas's mind against the popular commander in chief, his father's cousin the grand duke Nicholas, and on September 5, 1915, the emperor dismissed him, assuming supreme command himself. Since the emperor had no experience of war, almost all his ministers protested against this step as likely to impair the army's morale. A grotesque situation resulted: in the midst of a desperate struggle for national survival, competent ministers and officials were dismissed and replaced by worthless nominees of Rasputin. The court was widely suspected of treachery, and antidynastic feeling grew apace. Conservatives plotted Nicholas's deposition in the hope of saving the monarchy. Even the murder of Rasputin in December 1916 failed to dispel Nicholas's illusions: he blindly disregarded this ominous warning, as he did those by other highly placed personages, including members of his own family. Rasputin's murder merely strengthened Alexandra's resolve to uphold the principle of autocracy. Their isolation was virtually complete.

When riots broke out in Petrograd (St. Petersburg) on March 8, 1917, Nicholas instructed the city commandant to take firm measures and sent troops to restore order. It was too late. The government resigned, and the Duma, supported by the army, called on the emperor to abdicate. At Pskov on March 15, with fatalistic composure, Nicholas renounced the throne—not, as he had originally intended, in favour of his son, Alexis, but in favour of his brother Michael, who refused the crown.

Nicholas was detained at Tsarskoye Selo by Prince Lvov's provisional government. It was planned that he and his family would be sent to England; but instead, mainly because of the opposition of the Petrograd Soviet, the revolutionary Workers' and Soldiers' Council, they were removed to Tobolsk in Western Siberia. This step sealed their doom. In April 1918 they were taken to Yekaterinburg in the Urals.

When anti-Bolshevik "White" Russian forces approached the area, the local authorities were ordered to prevent a rescue, and on the night of July 16/17 the prisoners were all slaughtered in the cellar of the house where they had been confined. The bodies were burned, cast into an abandoned mine shaft, and then hastily buried elsewhere. A team of Russian scientists located the remains in 1976 but kept the discovery secret until after the collapse of the Soviet Union. By 1994 genetic analyses had positively identified the remains as those of Nicholas, Alexandra, three of their daughters (Anastasia, Tatiana, and Olga), and four servants. The remains were given a state funeral on July 17, 1998, and reburied in St. Petersburg in the crypt of the Cathedral of St. Peter and St. Paul. The remains of Alexis and Maria were not found until 2007, and the following year DNA testing confirmed their identity.

On August 20, 2000, the Russian Orthodox Church canonized the emperor and his family, designating them "passion bearers" (the lowest rank of sainthood) because of the piety they had shown during their final days. On October 1, 2008, Russia's Supreme Court ruled that the executions were acts of "unfounded repression" and granted the family full rehabilitation.

AGRARIAN REFORMS

The 1905 revolution showed that the village commune was not a guarantor of stability, as its protagonists had claimed, but rather an active promoter of unrest. Stolypin's attempt to undermine it was therefore part of his program for restoring order. But he had economic aims in mind as well. He aimed to give peasant households the chance to leave the commune and also to consolidate their strip holdings, enclosing them in one place as privately owned smallholdings in order to lay the basis for a prosperous peasant commercial agriculture.

The reforms, promoted energetically by the minister of agriculture, Aleksandr Vasilevich Krivoshein, enjoyed a tangible if not sensational measure of success. By 1915 some 20 percent of communal households had left the communes, and about 10 percent had taken the further step of consolidating their strips into one holding. All over the country, land settlement commissions were at work surveying, redrawing boundaries, and negotiating with the village assemblies on behalf of the new smallholders. Not unnaturally, individual withdrawals often aroused resentment, and the reform worked more effectively when whole villages agreed to consolidate and enclose their strips. Many households, both within and outside the commune, were joining cooperatives to purchase seeds and equipment or to market their produce. A good many peasants from the more densely settled regions of Russia were migrating to the open spaces of Siberia and northern Turkestan, whither Krivoshein attracted them by offering free land, subsidies for travel, and specialist advice. In nearly all categories, agricultural output rose sharply between 1906 and 1914, though in international grain markets Russia was beginning to lose ground to the United States, Canada, and Argentina.

While the non-Russian peoples had made considerable political and cultural gains in 1905–06, these were largely reversed after 1907. Ukrainian nationalism gained ground despite the efforts to suppress it and spread from its nucleus among the professional strata to embrace a growing number of both peasants and workers. In Poland, Russian was restored (after a brief interval in 1905–07) as the language of tuition in all schools, while local government assemblies were introduced with artificially inbuilt Russian majorities. The Finnish Diet, resisting a reduction in its powers, was reduced to the status of a provincial zemstvo, and Finland was submitted to direct rule from St. Petersburg.

Among Muslims the reform movement known as Jādid temporarily found an outlet for its political aspirations in the Muslim Group in the Duma. With the new electoral law of 1907, however, nearly all Muslims lost their representation in the house. Many of their leaders subsequently emigrated to Turkey, encouraged by the Young Turk Revolution of 1908. In Central Asia, industrialization and the increasing colonization of the grazing lands of the Turkic nomadic peoples by immigrants from European Russia caused bitter resentment and led to a widespread and violent rebellion that broke out in 1916.

WAR AND THE FALL OF THE MONARCHY

After 1906 Russia for some time had to pursue a cautious foreign policy in order to gain time to carry out reforms at home, to refit its army, and to rebuild its shattered navy. It set about these goals with the help of huge French loans that were contingent on the strengthening of the Franco-Russian alliance in both the diplomatic and military sense.

Excluded as a serious player in East Asia, Russia paid much more attention to the affairs of the Balkans, where the vulnerability of the Habsburg monarchy and that of the Ottoman Empire were generating an increasingly volatile situation. Besides, the Octobrists and many of the Rights who supported the government in the Duma took a great interest in the fate of the Slav nations of the region and favoured more active Russian support for them.

Operating from a position of weakness and under pressure from home, the Russian foreign minister, Aleksandr Petrovich Izvolsky, attempted to conclude a deal with his Austrian counterpart, Alois, Count Lexa von Aehrenthal, whereby Austria would occupy Bosnia and Herzegovina (over which it had exercised nominal suzerainty since 1878) in return for permitting a revision of the Straits Convention that would allow Russia to bring its warships out of the Black Sea if it were at war but Turkey were not. There was subsequent disagreement about what had been agreed, and, in the event, Austria occupied Bosnia and Herzegovina unilaterally, without making Russia any reciprocal concessions. Russia protested but was unable to achieve anything, as Germany threw its support unequivocally behind Austria.

Izvolsky had to resign after this public humiliation, and his successor, Sergey Dmitriyevich Sazonov, set about building an anti-Austrian bloc of Balkan states, including Turkey. This failed, but instead Russia was able to sponsor a Serbian-Greek-Bulgarian-Montenegrin alliance, which was successful in the First Balkan War against Turkey (1912–13). This seemed to herald a period of greater influence for Russia in the Balkans. Austria, however, reacted by demanding that the recently enlarged Serbia be denied an outlet to the Adriatic Sea by the creation of a new state of Albania. Russia supported the Serbian desire for an Adriatic port, but the European powers decided in favour of Austria. The Balkan alliance then fell apart, with Serbia and Greece fighting on the side of Turkey in the Second Balkan War (1913).

The assassination of Archduke Francis Ferdinand in June 1914 and the subsequent Austrian ultimatum to Serbia thus placed Russia in a very difficult situation. If Russia let Serbia down and yielded yet again to Austrian pressure, it would cease to be taken seriously as a participant in Balkan affairs and its prestige as a European great power would be seriously compromised. The alternative was to escalate the Balkan conflict to the point where Germany would come in behind Austria and a general European war would ensue. Understandably by the standards of the time, Russia chose the second alternative. Nicholas II hoped that, by mobilizing only those forces on his border with Austria-Hungary, he could avoid both German intervention and escalation into world war. The result, however, was World War I and the destruction of the monarchy in 1917.

The immediate effect of the outbreak of war was to strengthen social support for the monarchy. The Duma allowed its sessions to be suspended for some months, and a number of a voluntary organizations came into existence to lend support to the war effort. Zemstvo and Municipal unions were set up to coordinate medical relief, supplies, and transport. Unofficial War Industry Committees were established in major cities and some provinces to bring together representatives of local authorities, cooperatives, merchants, industrialists, and workers for mutual consultation on economic priorities. These were supplemented in the summer of 1915 by government-sponsored Special Councils in the fields of defense, transport, fuel, and food supplies. Civil society seemed to be maturing and diversifying as a result of the national emergency.

In 1914 the Franco-Russian alliance proved its value. The German army could have crushed either France or Russia alone but not both together. The Russian invasion of East Prussia

RUSSIAN SOLDIERS, WEARING WINTER UNIFORMS, ARE DEPICTED HERE AT THE GALICIAN FRONT IN POLAND IN DECEMBER 1914. IN THE EARLY MONTHS OF THE WAR, THE RUSSIANS ADVANCED IN GALICIA AFTER DEFEATING THE AUSTRO-HUNGARIAN ARMY, BUT THEY WERE FORCED TO RETREAT BY THE COMBINED GERMAN AND AUSTRO-HUNGARIAN OFFENSIVE IN THE SPRING AND SUMMER OF 1915.

in August 1914 was a failure: in two unsuccessful battles nearly 150,000 Russians were taken prisoner. The invasion did, however, cause the Germans to withdraw troops from their western front and thus enable the French to win the First Battle of the Marne (September 6–12, 1914). The entry of Turkey into the war on the side of Germany was a major setback, since it not only created a new front in the Caucasus (where the Russian armies performed rather well) but, by closing the straits, enormously reduced the supplies that the Allies could deliver to Russia. The failure of the British and French campaign in the Dardanelles and the entry of Bulgaria into the war on the German side meant that no relief could come from the south.

When the Central Powers launched a spring offensive in 1915, therefore, the Russian army was already short of munitions. The Germans and Austrians were able to occupy the whole of Poland and begin advancing into the western provinces and the Baltic region, unleashing a flood of refugees, who aggravated the already serious transport situation.

The military reverses of 1915, and especially the shortage of munitions, generated a strong swell of opinion in the Duma and State Council in favour of trying to compel the government to become more responsive to public opinion. The centre and left of the State Council combined with all the centre parties in the Duma, from the Moderate Rights to the Kadets, to form a Progressive Bloc. Its aim was to bring about the formation of a "government enjoying public confidence," whose ministers would be drawn, if possible, partly from the legislative chambers. The bloc called for a broad program of political reform, including the freeing of political prisoners, the repeal of discrimination against religious minorities, emancipation of the Jews, autonomy for Poland, elimination of the remaining legal disabilities suffered by peasants, repeal of anti-trade-union legislation, and democratization of local government. This program had the support of eight ministers, at least as a basis for negotiation, but not of the premier, Ivan Logginovich Goremykin, who regarded it as an attempt to undermine the autocracy.

The emperor did not approve of the Progressive Bloc either. For Nicholas, only the autocratic monarchy could sustain effective government and avoid social revolution and the disintegration of the multinational empire. He entertained quite different notions of how to deal with the crisis. In August 1915 he announced that he was taking personal command of the army, leaving the empress in charge of the government. He moved with his suite to Mogilyov, in Belarusia, where he remained until the revolution. However, he played only a ceremonial role, allowing his military chief of staff, General Mikhail Vasilyevich Alekseyev, to act as true commander in chief. During the next few months Nicholas dismissed all eight ministers who had supported the Progressive Bloc. Though he was unable to play the coordinating role that was so vital to the running of government, he still insisted that he was autocrat, maintaining ultimate power in his hands and preventing capable ministers from coordinating the administration of the government and war effort. From afar he ordained frequent pointless ministerial changes (dubbed by malicious gossip "ministerial leapfrog"), partly under the influence of his wife and Rasputin. Even loyal monarchists despaired of the situation, and in December 1916 Rasputin was murdered in a conspiracy involving some of them.

Ironically, the military situation improved greatly in 1916. The Polish and Baltic fronts were stabilized, and in 1916 General Aleksey Alekseyevich Brusilov launched a successful offensive in Galicia, took nearly 400,000 Austrian and German prisoners, and captured Chernovtsy (Czernowitz).

In the end it was the economic effect of the war that proved too much for the government. The shock of the munitions shortage prompted a partly successful reorganization of industry to concentrate on military production, and by late 1916 the army was better supplied than ever before. But life on the home front was grim. The German and Turkish blockade choked off most imports. The food supply was affected by the call-up of numerous peasants and by the diversion of transport to other needs. The strain of financing the war generated accelerating inflation, with which the pay of ordinary workers failed to keep pace. Strikes began in the summer of 1915 and increased during the following year, taking on an increasingly political tinge and culminating in a huge strike centred on the Putilov armament and locomotive works in Petrograd (the name given to St. Petersburg in August 1914) in January 1917.

THE RUSSIAN REVOLUTION OF 1917 AND THE TREATIES OF BREST-LITOVSK

The Russian Revolution of 1917 actually involved two revolutions, the first of which, in February (March, New Style) 1917, overthrew the imperial government and the second of which, in October (November, New Style), placed the Bolsheviks in power.

BROKEN BONDS AND THE INEVITABILITY OF REVOLUTION

By 1917 the bond between the tsar and most of the Russian people had been broken. Governmental corruption and inefficiency were rampant. The tsar's reactionary policies, including the occasional dissolution of the Duma, the chief fruit of the

1905 revolution, had spread dissatisfaction even to moderate elements. The Russian Empire's many ethnic minorities grew increasingly restive under Russian domination.

But it was the government's inefficient prosecution of World War I that finally provided the challenge the old regime could not meet. Ill equipped and poorly led, Russian armies suffered catastrophic losses in campaign after campaign against German armies. The war made revolution inevitable in two ways: it showed that Russia was no longer a military match for the nations of central and western Europe, and it hopelessly disrupted the economy. The government made matters worse by arresting all the members of the worker group of the Central War Industries Committee.

LAVR GEORGIYEVICH KORNILOV

Lavr Georgiyevich Kornilov was born on August 30 (August 18, Old Style), 1870, in Karkaralinsk, Western Siberia, (now Qargaraly, Kazakhstan). An imperial Russian general, Kornilov was accused of attempting to overthrow the Provisional Government established in Russia after the February Revolution of 1917 and to replace it with a military dictatorship.

An intelligence officer for the Imperial Russian Army during the Russo-Japanese War (1904–05) and a military attaché in Beijing (1907–11), Kornilov became a divisional commander during World War I. Captured by the Austrians at Przemysl (March 1915), he escaped in 1916 and was placed in command of an army corps.

After the February Revolution Kornilov was put in charge of the vital military district of Petrograd (St. Petersburg) by the provisional government. His determination to restore discipline and efficiency in the disintegrating Russian Army, however, made him unpopular in

(continued on the next page)

(continued from the previous page)

revolutionary Petrograd. He soon resigned, returned to the front, and participated in the abortive Russian offensive in June against the Germans in Galicia. On August 1 (July 18, Old Style), 1917, Prime Minister Aleksandr Kerensky appointed him commander in chief, but conflicts developed between Kornilov and Kerensky, owing to their opposing views on politics and on the role and nature of the Army. At the end of August, Kornilov sent troops toward Petrograd; Kerensky, interpreting this as an attempted military coup d'état, dismissed Kornilov and ordered him to come to Petrograd (August 27). Kornilov refused, and railroad workers prevented his troops from reaching their destination; on September 1 he surrendered and was imprisoned at Bykhov.

Kornilov later escaped, and, after the Bolsheviks seized power (October 1917), he assumed military command of the anti-Bolshevik ("White") volunteer army in the Don region. On April 13, 1918, he was killed during a battle for Ekaterinodar (now Krasnodar).

THE FEBRUARY REVOLUTION

The February (March, New Style) Revolution began among the food queues of the capital, Petrograd, which started calling for an end to autocracy. Riots over the scarcity of food broke out on February 24 (March 8). Soon workers from most of the major factories joined the demonstrations. The vital turning point came when Cossacks summoned to disperse the crowds refused to obey orders and troops in the city garrison mutinied and went over to the insurgents. The workers and soldiers rushed to re-create the institution they remembered from 1905, the Soviet of Workers' and Soldiers' Deputies. Soon their example was followed in many other towns and army units throughout the empire. Faced with the

WORKERS FROM A PUTILOV FACTORY IN ST. PETERSBURG STRIKE ON THE FIRST DAY OF THE FEBRUARY REVOLUTION IN 1917. THE PUTILOV COMPANY MADE VEHICLES FOR RAILWAYS AND BY 1917 BECAME THE MAJOR SUPPLIER OF ARTILLERY FOR THE RUSSIAN IMPERIAL ARMY.

threat of a civil war that would undermine the war effort, the military high command preferred to abandon Nicholas II in the hope that the Duma leaders would contain the revolution and provide effective leadership of the domestic front.

By agreement between the Petrograd soviet and the Duma, the Provisional Government was formed, headed by Prince Georgy Yevgenyevich Lvov (chairman of the Zemstvo Union) and consisting mainly of Kadets and Octobrists, though Aleksandr Fyodorovich Kerensky joined it from the Trudoviki. On

March 2 (March 15, New Style) 1917, this government's emissaries reached Pskov, where the emperor had become stranded in his train, attempting to reach Petrograd. He dictated to them his abdication, and when his brother, Grand Duke Michael, refused the throne, more than 300 years of rule by the Romanov dynasty came to an end.

A committee of the Duma appointed a Provisional Government to succeed the autocracy, but it faced a rival in the Petrograd Soviet of Workers' and Soldiers' Deputies. The 2,500 delegates to this soviet were chosen from factories and military units in and around Petrograd.

The Petrograd Soviet soon proved that it had greater authority than the Provisional Government, which sought to continue Russia's participation in the European war. On March 1 (March 14) the Petrograd Soviet issued its famous Order No. 1, which directed the military to obey only the orders of the soviet and not those of the Provisional Government. The Provisional Government was unable to countermand the order. All that now prevented the Petrograd Soviet from openly declaring itself the real government of Russia was fear of provoking a conservative coup.

Between March and October the Provisional Government was reorganized four times. The first government was composed entirely of liberal ministers, with the exception of the Socialist Revolutionary Aleksandr F. Kerensky. The subsequent governments were coalitions. None of them, however, was able to cope adequately with the major problems afflicting the country: peasant land seizures, nationalist independence movements in non-Russian areas, and the collapse of army morale at the front.

Meanwhile, soviets on the Petrograd model, in far closer contact with the sentiments of the people than the Provisional Government was, had been organized in cities and

ALEKSANDR FYODOROVICH KERENSKY

Born on April 22 (May 2, New Style), 1881, in Simbirsk (now Ulyanovsk), Russia, Aleksandr Fyodorovich Kerensky was a moderate socialist revolutionary who served as head of the Russian provisional government from July to October 1917 (Old Style).

While studying law at the University of St. Petersburg, Kerensky was attracted to the Narodniki (or populist) revolutionary movement. After graduating (1904), he joined the Socialist Revolutionary Party (c. 1905) and became a prominent lawyer, frequently defending revolutionaries accused of political offenses. In 1912 he was elected to the fourth Duma as a Trudoviki (Labour Group) delegate from Volsk (in Saratov province), and in the next several years he gained a reputation as an eloquent, dynamic politician of the moderate left.

Unlike some of the more radical socialists, he supported Russia's participation in World War I. He became increasingly disappointed with the tsarist regime's conduct of the war effort, however, and, when the February Revolution broke out in 1917, he urged the dissolution of the monarchy. He enthusiastically accepted the posts of vice chairman of the Petrograd Soviet of Workers' and Soldiers' Deputies and of minister of justice in the Provisional Government, formed by the Duma. The only person to hold positions in both governing bodies, he assumed the role of liaison between them. He instituted basic civil liberties—e.g., the freedoms of speech, press, assembly, and religion; universal suffrage; and equal rights for women—throughout Russia and became one of the most widely known and popular figures among the revolutionary leadership.

In May 1917, when a public uproar over the announcement of Russia's war aims (which Kerensky had approved) forced several ministers to resign, Kerensky was transferred to the posts

(continued on the next page)

(continued from the previous page)

of minister of war and of the navy and became the dominant personality in the new government. He subsequently planned a new offensive and toured the front, using his inspiring rhetoric to instill in the demoralized troops a desire to renew their efforts and defend the revolution. His eloquence, however, proved inadequate compensation for war weariness and lack of military discipline. Kerensky's June Offensive was an unmitigated failure.

When the Provisional Government was again compelled to reorganize in July 1917, Kerensky, who adhered to no rigid political dogma and whose dramatic oratorical style appeared to win him broad popular support, became prime minister. Despite his efforts to unite all political factions, he soon alienated the moderates and the officers' corps by summarily dismissing his commander in chief, General Lavr G. Kornilov, and personally replacing him (September); he also lost the confidence of the left wing by refusing to implement their radical social and economic programs and by apparently planning to assume dictatorial powers.

Consequently, when the Bolsheviks seized power in the October Revolution of 1917, Kerensky, who escaped to the front, was unable to gather forces to defend his government. He remained in hiding until May 1918, when he emigrated to western Europe and devoted himself to writing books on the revolution and editing émigré newspapers and journals. In 1940 he moved to the United States, where he lectured at universities and continued to write books on his revolutionary experiences. Kerensky died on June 11, 1970, in New York City.

major towns and in the army. In these soviets, "defeatist" sentiment, favouring Russian withdrawal from the war on almost any terms, was growing. One reason was that radical socialists increasingly dominated the soviet movement. At the First All-Russian Congress of Soviets, convened on June 3 (June

16), 1917, the Socialist Revolutionaries were the largest single bloc, followed by the Mensheviks and Bolsheviks.

Kerensky became head of the Provisional Government in July and put down a coup attempted by army commander in chief Lavr Georgiyevich Kornilov (according to some historians, Kerensky may have initially plotted with Kornilov in the hope of gaining control over the Petrograd Soviet). However, he was increasingly unable to halt Russia's slide into political, economic, and military chaos, and his party suffered a major split as the left wing broke from the Socialist Revolutionary Party. But while the Provisional Government's power waned, that of the soviets was increasing, as was the Bolsheviks' influence within them. By September the Bolsheviks and their allies, the Left Socialist Revolutionaries, had overtaken the Socialist Revolutionaries and Mensheviks and held majorities in both the Petrograd and Moscow soviets.

As Bolshevik domination grew in Petrograd, Moscow, and other major cities, the soviets accepted the idea that the revolution that would give them power would take place in two stages: the bourgeois, or middle-class, and the socialist. How long this transition period would last was a debatable point. The Mensheviks, the moderate socialists, held that Russia had to pass through its capitalist phase before the socialist one could appear. The Bolsheviks, the radical socialists, wanted the transition period to be short. Their firebrand leader, Lenin, sensed that power could be seized rather easily. The government was weak, and it could not rely on the army. With its large complement of peasants and workers in uniform, it was this group that formed the natural constituency of the socialists. Like the Mensheviks, the Socialist Revolutionaries, the main agrarian party, did not advocate a rush to power. More than 80 percent of the population lived in the countryside, a fact that made the

Socialist Revolutionaries certain to be the leading party when the Constituent Assembly was elected.

The Provisional Government was undone by war, economic collapse, and its own incompetence. Being a temporary administration, it postponed all hard decisions—what should be done about land seizures by the peasants, for example—for the Constituent Assembly. A fatal mistake by the government was its continued prosecution of the war. Middle-class politicians believed wrongly that one of the reasons for the February Revolution was popular anger at the incompetence of the conduct of the war. Disgruntled peasant-soldiers wanted to quit the army. They did not perceive Germany to be a threat to Russian sovereignty, and they deserted in droves to claim their piece of the landlord's estate. Industrial decline and rising inflation radicalized workers and cost the Provisional Government the needed support of the professional middle classes. The Bolshevik slogan of "All power to the soviets" was very attractive. Dual power prevailed. The government seemingly spoke for the country, but in reality it represented only the middle class; the soviets represented the workers and peasants. Moderate socialists—Mensheviks and Socialist Revolutionaries—dominated the Petrograd and Moscow soviets after February, but the radical Bolsheviks began to win local elections and by September had a majority in the Petrograd Soviet. By autumn the Bolshevik program of "peace, land, and bread" had won the party considerable support among the hungry urban workers and the soldiers, who were already deserting from the ranks in large numbers. Although a previous coup attempt (the July Days) had failed, the time now seemed ripe.

THE OCTOBER (NOVEMBER) REVOLUTION

One of the turning points in the struggle for power was the attempt by General Lavr Kornilov, who had been appointed commander in chief, to take control of Petrograd in August 1917 and wipe out the soviet. Aleksandr Kerensky, the prime minister, had been negotiating with Kornilov but then turned away and labeled Kornilov a traitor, perceiving his attack as a possible attempt to overthrow the government. Kerensky agreed to the arming of the Petrograd

This photograph from October 1917 shows an uprising in Moscow before the Kremlin and St. Basil's Cathedral. The Bolshevik coup initially encountered armed resistance in Moscow but the Bolsheviks prevailed.

Soviet, but after the failed coup the weapons were retained. The Bolsheviks could now consider staging an armed uprising. Had the Constituent Assembly been called during the summer, it could have undercut Lenin and his close colleague Leon Trotsky. Probably a majority of the population favoured state power passing to the soviets in October. They envisaged a broadly based socialist coalition government taking over. The October Revolution was precipitated by Kerensky himself when, angered by claims that the Bolsheviks controlled the Petrograd garrison, he sent troops to close down two Bolshevik newspapers. The Bolsheviks, led by Trotsky, feared that Kerensky would attempt to disrupt the Second All-Russian Congress, scheduled to open on October 25 (November 7, New Style); they reacted by sending troops to take over key communications and transportation points of the city. Lenin, who had been in hiding, appeared on the scene to urge the Bolsheviks to press forward and overthrow the Provisional Government, which they did on the morning of October 26. Kerensky tried to rally the armed forces to save his government but found no response among officers furious at his treatment of Kornilov. After the almost bloodless siege, Lenin proclaimed that power had passed to the soviets. The Congress of Soviets confirmed the transfer of power and passed several decrees submitted to it by Lenin, including one that socialized nonpeasant private land. It also formed a new provisional government, chaired by Lenin, that was to administer until the Constituent Assembly convened.

In Moscow the Bolshevik coup met with armed resistance from cadets and students, but they were eventually overcome. In the other cities of Russia soldiers, lured by Bolshevik slogans of immediate peace, crushed the opposition. The march to power was facilitated by the ambivalence of the Mensheviks and Socialists Revolutionaries who, though opposed to the October coup, feared a right-wing counterrevolution more than Bolshevism and discouraged physical resistance to it.

THE BOLSHEVIK DICTATORSHIP

Although Lenin and Trotsky had carried out the October coup in the name of soviets, they intended from the beginning to concentrate all power in the hands of the ruling organs of the Bolshevik Party. The resulting novel arrangement—the prototype of all totalitarian regimes—vested actual sovereignty in the hands of a private organization, called "the Party," which, however, exercised it indirectly, through state institutions. Bolsheviks held leading posts in the state: no decisions could be taken and no laws passed without their consent. The legislative organs, centred in the soviets, merely rubber-stamped Bolshevik orders. The state apparatus was headed by a cabinet called the Council of Peoples' Commissars (Sovnarkom), chaired by Lenin, all of whose members were drawn from the elite of the Party.

The Bolsheviks were solemnly committed to convening and respecting the will of the Constituent Assembly, which was to be elected in November 1917 on a universal franchise. Realizing that they had no chance of winning a majority, they procrastinated under various pretexts but eventually allowed the elections to proceed. The results gave a majority (40.4 percent) of the 41.7 million votes cast to the Socialists Revolutionaries. The Bolsheviks received 24 percent of the ballots. They allowed the assembly to meet for one day (January 5 [January 18, New Style], 1918) and then shut it down. The dispersal of the first democratically elected national legislature in Russian

THE BOLSHEVIK REVOLUTIONARY LEADERS VLADIMIR ILYICH LENIN (LEFT) AND LEON TROTSKY USED AS THEIR SLOGAN "ALL POWER TO THE SOVIETS!" IN NOVEMBER 1917 THE DELEGATES OF THE SECOND ALL-RUSSIAN CONGRESS OF SOVIETS ELECTED LENIN AS CHAIRMAN OF THE COUNCIL OF PEOPLE'S COMMISSARS, THE NEW SOVIET GOVERNMENT.

history marked the onset of the Bolshevik dictatorship. In the months that followed, one party after another was outlawed, non-Bolshevik newspapers and journals closed, and all overt opposition suppressed by a new secret police, the Cheka, which was given unlimited authority to arrest and shoot at its discretion suspected "counterrevolutionaries." The Peasant Union, representing four-fifths of the country's population, which had opposed the October coup, was subverted from within and replaced by an organization created and run by Bolsheviks.

The first and last coalition government remained in office only until March 1918, when, making great land concessions, the Bolsheviks accepted the defeatist Treaty of Brest-Litovsk, ending Russian participation in World War I.

TREATIES OF BREST-LITOVSK

The peace treaties signed at Brest-Litovsk (now in Belarus) by the Central Powers with the Ukrainian Republic (February 9, 1918) and with Soviet Russia (March 3, 1918) concluded hostilities between those countries during World War I. Peace negotiations, which the Soviet government had requested on November 8, 1917, began on December 22. They were divided into several sessions, during which the Soviet delegation tried to prolong the proceedings and took full advantage of its opportunity to issue propaganda statements, while the Germans grew increasingly impatient.

When no substantial progress had been made by January 18, 1918, the German general Max Hoffmann firmly presented the German demands, which included the establishment of independent states in the Polish and Baltic territories formerly belonging to the Russian Empire and in Ukraine. Leon Trotsky, head of the Soviet delegation since January 9, called for a recess (January 18–30). He returned to Petrograd, where he persuaded the reluctant Bolsheviks (including Lenin) to adopt a policy under which Russia would leave the war but sign no peace treaty ("neither war nor peace").

When negotiations resumed, the Soviet delegation again tried to stall; but after the Central Powers concluded a separate peace with the nationalist Ukrainian delegation (February 9), Trotsky announced the new Soviet policy. Negotiations came to a halt on February 10. But when the Germans renewed their military offensive (February 18), the Russians immediately requested that talks be resumed. On February 23, the Germans responded with an ultimatum allowing the Russians two days to open talks and three more to conclude them. Lenin, realizing that the new Soviet state was too weak to survive a continuation of the war, threatened to resign if the German terms were not met.

On March 3 the Soviet government accepted a treaty by which Russia lost Ukraine, its Polish and Baltic territories, and Finland. (Ukraine was recovered in 1919, during the Russian Civil War.) The treaty was ratified by the Congress of Soviets on March 15, 1918. (Both the Ukrainian and Russian treaties were annulled by the Armistice on November 11, 1918, which marked the Allied defeat of Germany. By the terms of the Treaty of Versailles Germany had to renounce what it had gained at Brest-Litovsk.)

Soviets under control by the summer of 1918. Local soviets continued to defy the Bolsheviks but to no avail. Democracy received little nurturing and was never institutionalized; politics remained personalized. The cult of the strong leader gradually emerged, with local "Lenins" cropping up throughout the land.

In March 1918 the Bolshevik Party was renamed the Russian Communist Party (Bolshevik) in order to distinguish it from Social Democratic parties in Russia and Europe and to separate the followers of Lenin from those affiliated with the non-revolutionary Socialist International. The party was directed by a Central Committee. To streamline work, from March 1919 onward its management was entrusted to the Secretariat, the Organizational Bureau (Orgburo), and the Political Bureau (Politburo). The Secretariat and Orgburo dealt largely with personnel matters, while the Politburo combined legislative and executive powers.

CIVIL WAR AND WAR COMMUNISM

One side can start a war, but it takes two to end one. The Bolsheviks found that this principle applied to them after October, when they expected to disengage quickly from World War I. Of the three points of their effective slogan—"Peace, land, and bread"—the first proved to be the most difficult to realize.

WAR OR PEACE?

Trotsky, the silver-tongued Bolshevik negotiator, had lectured the Germans and Austrians on Georg Hegel's philosophy and other abstruse subjects at Brest-Litovsk. He thought that he had time on his side. He was waiting for news of revolution in Berlin and Vienna. It never came, and the Bolsheviks found

THIS SOVIET PROPAGANDA POSTER FROM THE 1920S EXCLAIMS "ALL POWER TO THE SOVIETS! PEACE TO THE PEOPLE! LAND TO THE PEASANTS! FACTORIES AND MILLS TO THE WORKERS!"

themselves at the Germans' mercy. The issue of peace or war tore the Bolsheviks apart. Lenin favoured peace at any price, believing that it was purely an interim settlement before inevitable revolution. Nikolay Bukharin, a left-wing Bolshevik in the early Soviet period, wanted revolutionary war, while Trotsky wanted neither war nor peace. Trotsky believed the Germans did not have the military muscle to advance, but they did, and eventually the very harsh peace of the Brest-Litovsk treaty was imposed on Russia. The Socialist Revolutionaries left the coalition, and some resorted to terrorism, the target being the Bolshevik leadership. Ukraine slipped under German influence, and the Mensheviks held sway in the Caucasus. Only part of Russia—Moscow, Petrograd, and much of the industrial heartland—was under Bolshevik control. The countryside belonged to the Socialist Revolutionaries. Given the Bolshevik desire to dominate the whole of Russia and the rest of the former tsarist empire, civil war was inevitable.

LEON TROTSKY

Leon Trotsky was the byname of Lev Davidovich Bronshtein, who was born on November 7 [October 26, Old Style], 1879, in Yanovka, Ukraine, and died on August 21, 1940, in Coyoacán, Mexico). Trotsky was a communist theorist and agitator, a leader in Russia's October Revolution in 1917, and later commissar of foreign affairs and of war in the Soviet Union (1917–24). In the struggle for power following Vladimir Ilyich Lenin's death, however, Joseph Stalin emerged as victor, while Trotsky was removed from all positions of power and later exiled (1929). He remained the leader of an anti-Stalinist opposition abroad until his assassination by a Stalinist agent.

Trotsky's father, David Bronshtein, was a farmer of Russified Jewish background who had settled as a colonist in the steppe region, and his mother, Anna, was of the educated middle class. He had an older brother and sister; two other siblings died in infancy. At the age of eight, he was sent to school in Odessa, where he spent eight years with the family of his mother's nephew, a liberal intellectual. When he moved to Nikolayev in 1896 to complete his schooling, he was drawn into an underground socialist circle and introduced to Marxism. After briefly attending the University of Odessa, he returned to Nikolayev to help organize the underground South Russian Workers' Union.

Arrested in January 1898 for revolutionary activity, Bronshtein spent four and a half years in prison and in exile in Siberia, during which time he married his coconspirator Aleksandra Sokolovskaya and fathered two daughters. He escaped in 1902 with a forged passport bearing the name Trotsky, which he adopted as his revolutionary pseudonym. His wife remained behind, and the separation became permanent. Trotsky made his way to London, where he joined the group of Russian Social Democrats working with Vladimir Ulyanov (Lenin) on the revolutionary newspaper *Iskra* ("The Spark").

At the Second Congress of the Russian Social-Democratic Workers' Party, held in Brussels and London in July 1903, Trotsky sided with the Menshevik faction—advocating a democratic approach to socialism—against Lenin and the Bolsheviks. Shortly before this, in Paris, Trotsky had met and married Natalya Sedova, by whom he subsequently had two sons, Lev and Sergey.

Upon the outbreak of revolutionary disturbances in 1905, Trotsky returned to Russia. He became a leading spokesman of the St. Petersburg Soviet (council) of Workers' Deputies when it organized a revolutionary strike movement and other measures of defiance against the tsarist government. In the aftermath, Trotsky was jailed and brought to trial in 1906. While incarcerated, Trotsky wrote one of his major works, "Results and Prospects," setting forth his theory of permanent revolution.

(continued on the next page)

(continued from the previous page)

In 1907, after a second exile to Siberia, Trotsky once again escaped. He settled in Vienna and supported himself as a correspondent in the Balkan Wars of 1912–13. At the outbreak of World War I, Trotsky joined the majority of Russian Social Democrats who condemned the war and refused to support the war effort of the tsarist regime. He moved to Switzerland and then to Paris. His antiwar stance led to his expulsion from both France and Spain. He reached New York City in January 1917, where he joined the Bolshevik theoretician Nikolay Bukharin in editing the Russian-language paper *Novy Mir* ("The New World").

Trotsky hailed the outbreak of revolution in Russia in February (March, New Style) as the opening of the permanent revolution he had predicted. He reached Petrograd in mid-May and assumed the leadership of a left-wing Menshevik faction. Following the abortive July Days uprising, Trotsky was arrested in the crackdown on the Bolshevik leadership carried out by Aleksandr Kerensky's liberal government. In August, while still in jail, Trotsky was formally admitted to the Bolshevik Party and was also elected to membership on the Bolshevik Central Committee. He was released from prison in September and shortly afterward was elected chairman of the Petrograd Soviet of Workers' and Soldiers' Deputies.

When fighting was precipitated by an ineffectual government raid early on November 6 (October 24, Old Style), Trotsky took a leading role in directing countermeasures for the soviet, while reassuring the public that his Military Revolutionary Committee meant only to defend the Congress of Soviets. Governmental authority crumbled quickly, and Petrograd was largely in Bolshevik hands by the time Lenin reappeared from the underground on November 7 to take direct charge of the Revolution and present the Congress of Soviets with an accomplished fact when it convened next day.

Trotsky continued to function as the military leader of the Revolution when Kerensky vainly attempted to retake Petrograd with loyal troops. He organized and supervised the forces that broke Kerensky's efforts at the Battle of Pulkovo on November 13. Immediately afterward he joined Lenin in defeating proposals for a coalition government including Mensheviks and Socialist Revolutionaries.

As foreign commissar, Trotsky's first charge was to implement the Bolsheviks' program of peace by calling for immediate armistice negotiations among the warring powers. Germany and its allies responded, and in mid-December peace talks were begun at Brest-Litovsk, though Trotsky continued vainly to invite support from the Allied governments. In January 1918 Trotsky entered into the peace negotiations personally and shocked his adversaries by turning the talks into a propaganda forum. He then recessed the talks and returned to Petrograd to argue against acceptance of Germany's annexationist terms, even though Lenin had meanwhile decided to pay the German price for peace and thus buy time for the Soviet state. Between Lenin's position and Bukharin's outright call for revolutionary war, Trotsky proposed the formula "no war, no peace." When the Germans resumed their offensive in mid-February, the Bolshevik Central Committee was compelled to make a decision; Trotsky and his followers abstained from the vote, and Lenin's acceptance of the German terms was endorsed.

Following the conclusion of the Treaty of Brest-Litovsk, Trotsky resigned as foreign commissar, turning the office over to Georgy Chicherin and was immediately made commissar of war, theretofore a committee responsibility. As war commissar, Trotsky faced the formidable task of building a new Red Army out of the shambles of the old Russian army and preparing to defend the communist government against the imminent threats of civil war and foreign intervention. Trotsky chose to concentrate on developing a small but disciplined and professionally competent force. His abandonment of the revolutionary ideal of democratization and guerrilla tactics prompted much criticism of his methods among other communists. He was particularly criticized for recruiting former tsarist officers ("military specialists") and putting them to work under the supervision of communist military

(continued on the next page)

(continued from the previous page)

commissars. Trotsky's military policies were resisted unsuccessfully by a coalition of ultraleft purists and rival party leaders, notably Stalin, with whom Trotsky had an acrimonious clash over the defense of the city of Tsaritsyn (later Stalingrad, now Volgograd). Trotsky's approach was, however, vindicated by the success of the Red Army in turning back attacks by the anticommunist White armies in 1918 and 1919.

With the triumph of the communist forces and the end of the Russian Civil War in 1920, Trotsky, retaining his office as commissar of war, turned his attention to the economic reconstruction of Russia. He first proposed a relaxation of the stringent centralization of War Communism to allow market forces to operate. Rejected in this, he endeavoured to apply military discipline to the economy, using soldiers as labour armies and attempting to militarize the administration of the transportation system.

During the civil war and War Communism phase of the Soviet regime, Trotsky was clearly established as the number-two man next to Lenin. He was one of the initial five members of the Politburo when that top Communist Party policy-making body was created in 1919. In intellectual power and administrative effectiveness, he was Lenin's superior and did not hesitate to disagree with him, but he lacked facility in political manipulation to win party decisions. Trotsky took a prominent part in the launching of the Comintern in 1919 and wrote its initial manifesto.

In the winter of 1920–21 widespread dissension broke out over the policies of War Communism, not only among the populace but among the party leadership as well. The point at issue in the controversy was the future role of the trade unions. The utopian left wing wanted the unions to administer industry; Lenin and the cautious wing wanted the unions confined to supervising working conditions; Trotsky and his supporters tried to reconcile radicalism and pragmatism by visualizing administration through unions representing the central state authority.

As commissar of war, Leon Trotsky (front centre) frequently visited his troops. Trotsky is seen here in 1921 reviewing the Red Army in Moscow.

The crisis came to a head in March 1921, with agitation for democracy within the party on the one hand and armed defiance represented by the naval garrison at Kronshtadt on the other. At this point Trotsky sided with Lenin, commanding the forces that suppressed the Kronshtadt Rebellion and backing the suppression of open factional activity in the party. Trotsky accepted Lenin's retreat from ideal communism in favour of the New Economic Policy, including his conventional view of the trade unions. This degree of accord, however, did not prevent Trotsky from losing a substantial degree of political influence at the 10th Party Congress in March 1921.

When Lenin was stricken with his first cerebral hemorrhage in May 1922, the question of eventual succession to the leadership of

(continued on the next page)

(continued from the previous page)

Russia became urgent. Trotsky, owing to his record and his charismatic qualities, was the obvious candidate in the eyes of the party rank and file, but jealousy among his colleagues on the Politburo prompted them to combine against him. As an alternative, the Politburo supported the informal leadership of the troika composed of Grigory Zinovyev, Lev Kamenev, and Stalin.

In the winter of 1922–23 Lenin recovered partially and turned to Trotsky for assistance in correcting the errors of the troika, particularly in foreign trade policy, the handling of the national minorities, and reform of the bureaucracy. In December 1922, warning in his then secret "Testament" of the danger of a split between Trotsky and Stalin, Lenin characterized Trotsky as a man of "exceptional abilities" but "too far-reaching self-confidence and a disposition to be too much attracted by the purely administrative side of affairs." Just before he was silenced by a final stroke in March 1923, Lenin invited Trotsky to open an attack on Stalin, but Trotsky chose to bide his time, possibly contemplating an alliance against Zinovyev. Stalin moved rapidly to consolidate his hold on the Central Committee at the 12th Party Congress in April 1923.

By fall, alarmed by inroads of the secret police among party members and efforts to weaken his control of the war commissariat, Trotsky decided to strike out against the party leadership. In October he addressed a wide-ranging critique to the Central Committee, stressing especially the violation of democracy in the party and the failure to develop adequate economic planning. Reforms were promised, and Trotsky responded with an open letter detailing the direction they should take. This, however, served only as the signal for a massive propaganda counterattack against Trotsky and his supporters on grounds of factionalism and opportunism. At this critical moment Trotsky fell ill of an undiagnosed fever and could take no personal part in the struggle. Because of Stalin's organizational controls, the party leadership easily won, and the "New Course" controversy was terminated at the 13th Party Conference in January 1924 (the first substantially stage-managed party assembly) with the condemnation of the Trotsky-ist opposition as a Menshevik-like illegal factional deviation. Lenin's death a week later only confirmed Trotsky's isolation. Convalescing on the Black Sea coast, Trotsky was deceived about the date of the funeral, failed to return to Moscow, and left the scene to Stalin.

Attacks on Trotsky did not cease. When the 13th Party Congress, in May 1924, repeated the denunciations of his violations of party discipline, Trotsky vainly professed his belief in the omnipotence of the party. The following fall he took a different tack in his essay "The Lessons of October 1917," linking the opposition of Zinovyev and Kamenev to the October Revolution with the failure of the Soviet-inspired German communist uprising in 1923. The party leadership replied with a wave of denunciation, counterposing Trotskyism to Leninism, denigrating Trotsky's role in the Revolution, and denouncing the theory of permanent revolution as a Menshevik heresy. In January 1925 Trotsky was removed from the war commissariat.

Early in 1926, following the split between the Stalin-Bukharin leadership and Zinovyev-Kamenev group and the denunciation of the latter at the 14th Party Congress, Trotsky joined forces with his old adversaries Zinovyev and Kamenev to resume the political offensive. For a year and a half this "United Opposition" grasped at every opportunity to put its criticisms before the party membership, despite the increasingly severe curbs being placed on such discussion. Again they stressed the themes of party democracy and economic planning, condemned the leadership's concessions to bourgeois elements, and denounced Stalin's theory of "socialism in one country" as a pretext for abandoning world revolution.

The response of the leadership was a rising tide of official denunciation, supplemented by an anti-Semitic whispering campaign. In October 1926 Trotsky was expelled from the Politburo, and a year later he and Zinovyev were dropped from the Central Committee. After an abortive attempt at a demonstration on the 10th anniversary of the Revolution, the two were expelled from the party.

(continued on the next page)

(continued from the previous page)

In January 1928 Trotsky and his principal followers were exiled to remote parts of the Soviet Union, Trotsky himself being assigned to Alma-Ata (now Almaty) in Central Asia. In January 1929 Trotsky was banished from the territory of the Soviet Union. He was initially received by the government of Turkey and domiciled on the island of Prinkipo. He plunged into literary activity there and completed his autobiography and his history of the Russian Revolution.

In 1933 Trotsky secured permission to move to France. After Hitler's victory in Germany, Trotsky gave up the hope of reforming the Communist International and called on his followers to establish their own revolutionary parties and form a Fourth International. This movement (whose American branch was the Socialist Workers' Party) proved to be little more than a shadow organization, although a small founding conference was officially held in France in 1938.

In 1935 Trotsky was compelled to move to Norway, and in 1936, under Soviet pressure, he was forced to seek asylum in Mexico, where he settled at Coyoacán. He was represented as the principal conspirator, in absentia, in the treason trials of former communist opposition leaders held in Moscow (1936–38). The evidence of treasonable plotting, however, was later proved to be fictitious.

In May 1940, men armed with machine guns attacked his house, but Trotsky survived. Some three months later, however, Ramón Mercader, a Spanish communist who had won the confidence of the Trotsky household, fatally struck him with an ice pick. The Soviet government disclaimed any responsibility, and Mercader was sentenced to the maximum 20-year term under Mexican law.

Trotsky was undoubtedly the most brilliant intellect brought to prominence by the Russian Revolution, outdistancing Lenin and other theoreticians both in the range of his interests and in the imaginativeness of his perceptions. He was an indefatigable worker, a rousing public speaker, and a decisive administrator. On the other hand, Trotsky was not successful as a leader of men, partly because he allowed his brilliance and arrogance to antagonize the lesser lights in the communist movement. Perhaps he fatally compromised himself when he became a Bolshevik in 1917, subordinating himself to Lenin's leadership and accepting the methods of dictatorship that he had previously condemned. Had Trotsky won the struggle to succeed Lenin, the character of the Soviet regime would almost certainly have been substantially different, particularly in foreign policy, cultural policy, and the extent of terroristic repression. Trotsky's failure, however, seems to have been almost inevitable, considering his own qualities and the conditions of authoritarian rule by the Communist Party organization.

THE CIVIL WAR (1918-20)

The Red Army was formed in February 1918, and Trotsky became its leader. He was to reveal great leadership and military skill, fashioning a rabble into a formidable fighting force. The Reds were opposed by the "Whites," anticommunists led by former imperial officers. There were also the "Greens" and the anarchists, who fought the Reds and were strongest in Ukraine; the anarchists' most talented leader was Nestor Makhno. The Allies (Britain, the United States, Italy, and a host of other states) intervened on the White side and provided much matériel and finance. The Bolsheviks controlled the industrial heartland of Russia, and their lines of communication were short. Those of the Whites, who were dispersed all the way to the Pacific, were long. The Reds recruited many ex-tsarist officers but also produced many of their own. By mid-1920 the Reds had consolidated their hold on the country.

ADMIRAL ALEKSANDR VASILYEVICH KOLCHAK, LEADER OF THE WHITE ARMY, REVIEWS HIS TROOPS IN THE FALL OF 1919, DURING THE RUSSIAN CIVIL WAR. IN 1919-1920, KOLCHAK WAS RECOGNIZED BY THE WHITES AS THE SUPREME RULER OF RUSSIA.

The feat of winning the civil war and the organizational methods adopted to do so made a deep impact on Bolshevik thinking. Joseph Stalin, a party leader, talked about the party in terms of an army. There were political fronts, economic struggles, campaigns, and so on. The Bolsheviks were ruthless in their pursuit of victory. The Cheka (a forerunner of the notorious KGB), or political police, was formed in December 1917 to protect communist power. By the end of the civil war the Cheka had become a powerful force.

POLISH-BORN FELIKS EDMUNDOVICH DZERZHINSKY (SEATED, CENTRE) IS SHOWN HERE WITH UKRAINIAN MEMBERS OF CHEKA, THE BOLSHEVIK SECRET POLICE, IN 1920. DZERZHINSKY PLAYED AN ACTIVE ROLE IN THE REVOLUTION OF 1917, WAS NAMED HEAD OF THE CHEKA, AND ORGANIZED THE FIRST CONCENTRATION CAMPS IN RUSSIA.

Among the targets of the Cheka were Russian nationalists, who objected strongly to the bolshevization of Russia. They regarded bolshevism as alien and based on western European and not Russian norms. Lenin was always mindful of "Great Russian" chauvinism, which was one reason he never permitted the formation of a separate Russian Communist Party apart from that of the Soviet Union. Russia, alone of the U.S.S.R.'s 15 republics, did not have its own communist party. It was belatedly founded in 1990.

VLADIMIR ILYICH LENIN

Few individuals in modern history had as profound an effect on their times or evoked as much heated debate as the Russian revolutionary Vladimir Ilyich Lenin. To his supporters, Lenin appeared as the individual who, through the sheer force of his will and dedication to the revolutionary struggle, played the decisive role in the Russian Revolution of 1917 that brought about the first government dedicated to overturning the political and economic system of Western capitalism. His detractors denounced Lenin as an antidemocratic despot who, through the use of bloody repression and indiscriminate terror, laid the foundation for the first modern totalitarian police state.

Lenin's birth name was Vladimir Ilyich Ulyanov. He was born on April 22 (April 10, Old Style), 1870, the third of five children of a well-to-do Russian family. The Ulyanovs resided in Simbirsk, Russia, a small town on the Volga River. Ilya Ulyanov, Vladimir's father, served as a high-level education bureaucrat in the tsar's government. No outward signs existed to indicate that each of the children from this respectable family would shun the path of bureaucratic life and enter into the burgeoning ranks of the Russian revolutionary movement—none of them with more vehemence than Vladimir and his older brother Aleksandr.

The death of Ilya Ulyanov in 1886 was followed by an even greater family tragedy. In March 1887, the tsarist secret police arrested Aleksandr Ulyanov. Aleksandr, a bright and introverted chemistry student at the University of St. Petersburg (now St. Petersburg State University; from 1924 to 1991 Leningrad State University), was charged with conspiring, along with members of the radical revolutionary group Narodnaya Volya (People's Will), to assassinate Tsar Alexander III. Following a brief trial that clearly exposed Aleksandr's role in the plot, Aleksandr was found guilty and promptly executed.

By his own admission, the unexpected arrest and execution of his older brother had a profound influence on Vladimir Ulyanov. Vladimir had shown no previous proclivity for politics, let alone revolutionary politics, but he became determined to understand what factors and ideas had prompted his brother to sacrifice his life willingly for the revolutionary struggle. The 17-year-old Vladimir immersed himself in books and journals from his brother's collection, devouring the writings of such radical Russian political thinkers as Nikolay Chernyshevsky and Dmitry Pisarev, two of the most prominent writers who inspired a generation of young Russian "populist" intellectuals to dedicate themselves to the overthrow of the tsarist autocracy and to the establishment of an egalitarian socialist society.

Several months after the death of Aleksandr, Vladimir enrolled at Kazan University (now Kazan Federal University) to study law. As the brother of a now-famous revolutionary martyr, he was greeted warmly by members of the revolutionary underground and watched closely by the tsar's secret police. In December 1887 officials from the school expelled him for his role in a student demonstration, and he returned home to live with his family. During the ensuing three years,

(continued on the next page)

(continued from the previous page)

he read voluminously, studying law, languages, and, most significantly, the writings of Karl Marx. Ulyanov became a firm convert to Marx's class-struggle–based interpretation of history.

In 1895, following a brief journey to Europe, Ulyanov returned to St. Petersburg, where he also returned to the revolutionary underground. In 1897 he was arrested for spreading propaganda among workers in St. Petersburg and exiled to Siberia. While in Siberia, Ulyanov married Nadezhda Krupskaya, a fellow Marxist whom he had known from his time in St. Petersburg. Ulyanov spent his years in Siberia compiling his first formidable work, *The Development of Capitalism in Russia* (published legally in 1899), which attempted to place Russia's historical development within the context of Marx's political and economic theories. Ulyanov served his exile in a town near the Lena River, and it was from the name of this river that he took the pseudonym that would remain with him until the end of his days.

In 1900, Lenin and Krupskaya were released from exile. Lenin returned briefly to St. Petersburg, only to find that the burgeoning Marxist movement that he had left in 1897 was beset by ideological squabbles. Eager to reestablish unity among the Russian Marxists, Lenin and his wife traveled to Geneva, Switzerland, where they sought out the foremost Russian Marxist revolutionary group, headed by the so-called father of Russian Marxism, Georgy Plekhanov. Lenin proposed that the Geneva expatriates publish a new journal, known as *Iskra* ("The Spark"), to serve as a mouthpiece for orthodox Marxist theories. The editorial staff was composed of some of the most prominent members of the Russian Marxist intelligentsia: Plekhanov, Vera Zasulich, Pavel Akselrod, L. Martov, Leon Trotsky, and Lenin. Each of these individuals would play prominent roles in the revolutionary struggles of the early 20th century.

From the outset, the *Iskra* group faced internal differences. These divisions came to the forefront in 1903, when the *Iskra* group organized a conference of Russia's various Marxist revolutionary groups with the intention of unifying the Marxist movement into one social democratic party. At that meeting, which began in Belgium but transferred to London, England, following a police raid, the *Iskra* group, as well as the entire Russian Social-Democratic Workers' party, split into two different ideological camps. Lenin played the decisive role in driving a wedge between the two factions when he proposed that the Russian Social-Democratic Workers' party should organize itself as a small, conspiratorial revolutionary vanguard that would lead the mass of the Russian working class toward revolution. The opposition group, headed by Martov, demanded the creation of a mass-based, openly democratic Social Democratic party. Plekhanov, himself no great defender of democracy, supported Lenin's faction, but the remainder of the *Iskra* group sided with Martov and attacked Lenin harshly for his dictatorial instincts. Martov's faction, which held a majority throughout most of the conference, lost the deciding vote on party organization after several delegates to the conference walked out in protest of the proceedings. Lenin's radical faction barely won the crucial vote, and Lenin claimed for his group the name Bolsheviks ("One of the Majority"). Martov's group, which would hold the majority within the divided Social Democratic party until mid-1917, nevertheless accepted the moniker of Mensheviks ("Those of the Minority").

In Russia, the divisions between the two Social Democratic parties remained blurred until 1917. From 1903 until 1914, the two groups worked side by side, attempting to recruit workers to the Social Democratic cause. Throughout much of this period, Lenin lived with his wife as a wandering exile, traveling and residing throughout Europe. Lenin returned to Russia briefly following the outbreak of revolution in 1905, but he stayed less than two years before returning to Europe. Despite his removal from the ground-level struggle, Lenin continued to issue decrees on policies for the Bolshevik faction of the Social Democratic party. Lenin attacked many of his Menshevik opponents for suggesting that the Social Democrats should concentrate only on such legal activities as trade union activism and distribution of Socialist propaganda.

(continued on the next page)

THE RUSSIAN REVOLUTION
THE FALL OF THE TSARS AND THE RISE OF COMMUNISM

(continued from the previous page)

While Lenin and his Bolshevik faction publicly denounced the use of terrorism as a political tactic, members of the Bolshevik faction nevertheless engaged in several assassinations of tsarist officials, and the Bolsheviks regularly resorted to bank robberies to fill the party coffers. Lenin's radical rhetoric and tactics brought him the scorn of his opponents in the Social Democratic party, and the split between the Mensheviks and Bolsheviks became more acute.

Lenin and Krupskaya were in Switzerland when World War I broke out in August 1914. No issue divided the members of the Russian Social Democrats as decisively as did the outbreak of the war. The response of Socialists throughout Europe varied greatly. As hostilities mounted prior to the outbreak of war, members of the international Social Democratic movement demanded peace. Once war became imminent, the facade of an international movement fell to pieces. Socialists throughout Europe were swept up in the outpouring of patriotism that occurred at the outset of the war. Among the Russian Social Democrats, the enthusiasm for war was far less pervasive. The bulk of the Socialists continued to call for peace without indemnities. Lenin, however, was the only prominent Russian Socialist to take an even more radical stance on the war. He denounced it as a conflict of competing imperialist powers, and he called on the working peoples of all nations to instead use their weapons to overthrow their capitalist governments.

Initially, Lenin's call for class-based civil war fell on deaf ears in Russia. As the war dragged on and as the vast casualties mounted, the mood of the Russian working class and peasantry became more inflammatory. Strikes, which had ceased at the outbreak of war, resumed during 1915 and 1916. In March (February according to the Old Style calendar) 1917, spontaneous revolution broke out in Petrograd (which had been renamed from St. Petersburg at the beginning of World War I), and Tsar Nicholas II was forced to abdicate. The new Provisional Government—composed of a coalition of conservative, liberal, and moderate socialist politicians—made clear their

100

intention to continue the war at all costs. Lenin, still in Switzerland, increased his attack on the new Provisional Government, and he sought to return to Russia in the hopes of fomenting revolution.

The German government, eager to remove Russia from the war and to consequently eliminate the burdensome eastern front, saw in Lenin a potentially potent and corrosive weapon to release on their Russian opponents. Lenin was provided with funds from the German government and sent in a sealed train car back to Russia. Because of this German assistance, his critics would later argue that Lenin was ostensibly a German agent, willing to accept German support and funds to undermine the Russian war effort. While it is clear that Lenin proved willing to use German support to promote the radicalization of the revolution in Russia, it is equally clear that Lenin intended, once in power, to assist German socialists in fomenting an equally radical revolution in Germany.

Lenin arrived in Russia on April 16, 1917. On the following day Trotsky—who had broken with the Mensheviks and become Lenin's most trusted and capable ally—arrived in Russia. The two men, both powerful orators, immediately sounded the call for the end of hostilities and for the beginning of class war in Russia. Lenin's following increased dramatically during the summer of 1917, as a long-anticipated Russian counteroffensive collapsed completely, resulting in some 200,000 casualties. Lenin's call for peace won more and more converts. In July 1917, workers and soldiers stationed in Petrograd took to the streets, demanding that the government turn control over to the revolutionary Workers' and Soldiers' Soviets, or councils, which were sympathetic to the Bolsheviks. The government issued a warrant for Lenin's arrest, and he fled to Finland.

Lenin returned to Russia in disguise at the end of October. On the evening of November 6 (October 24 according to the Old Style calendar), 1917, the Bolsheviks, meeting in secret, resolved to overtake the government and establish a new Provisional Government. Unlike the revolution of February, the October Revolution occurred

(continued on the next page)

THE RUSSIAN REVOLUTION
THE FALL OF THE TSARS AND THE RISE OF COMMUNISM

(continued from the previous page)

with barely any mass uprising. Red Army troops under the direction of Trotsky launched attacks on key installations throughout Petrograd during the evening, culminating in a march on the government's Winter Palace. By the morning of November 7, the city of Petrograd was in Bolshevik hands.

Following the pacification of Russia's major cities, Lenin declared the formation of the world's first Communist government. Opposition groups were banned, and newspapers and journals of other political groups were shut down. Banks and industries throughout the country were placed under the control of the new government. The Bolshevik government outlawed trade and the ownership of most private property. Lenin, convinced of the possibility of forcing social change on the Russian population, argued that the severe measures would facilitate the immediate transition to socialism in Russia. His numerous Socialist opponents—led by his one-time allies Martov, Plekhanov, and Akselrod—insisted that Lenin failed to understand the basic fundamentals of the theories of Marx, in whose name he had purportedly made the Bolshevik Revolution. Russia, they argued, was simply not ready to make the jump to socialism. Such a misguided experiment, they warned, would end in dictatorship.

Lenin dismissed his critics' warnings and set out to make good on his promise for peace. He immediately opened negotiations with Germany to end the war between the two nations. The German government, with its army poised to march undeterred on Russia, demanded exorbitant concessions from Lenin's government, including the Russian territories of Poland, the Caucasus, and Ukraine. When the terms of the proposed peace agreement became known, Lenin's political opponents accused the Bolsheviks of outright treason. In March 1918 the Bolshevik government, with its Russian and German opponents at its throat, hesitatingly signed the Brest-Litovsk peace agreement, ending the war with Germany.

The signing of the Brest-Litovsk treaty sparked civil war in Russia. Lenin's political opponents, including tsarist loyalists, various socialist factions, and many liberal groups, headed to the south of the country. Civil war raged for three years as the two armies—Lenin's Red Army and the White Army of the opposition—vied for control of the country. Lenin instituted a series of drastic and radical measures, known as War Communism, designed to aid the Red Army war effort against the Whites. Groups of armed brigades were sent to the countryside to appropriate by force food from the peasantry; a new secret police, named the Cheka, was formed by Lenin to weed out criminals, political opponents, and "counterrevolutionary" agitators. In July 1918, the Bolshevik government issued the most notorious of its edicts when, fearing a promonarchist backlash, it ordered Red Army troops to carry out the murder of Nicholas II and his entire family.

Throughout the course of the civil war, both the White and Red armies carried out atrocities against their perceived opponents. Once in power, neither Lenin nor his fellow Bolsheviks hesitated to use indiscriminate violence as a means of quashing rebellion and extending the power and influence of the Bolshevik government. Lenin called the violent tactics the "Red Terror," and he vowed to destroy enemies of the state, both real and perceived. The exact number of victims who fell before the Red Terror—many of whom were shot en masse without trial or evidence—remains unknown. Estimates of the human toll of the Red Terror range from roughly 13,000 to more than 140,000. Both Lenin and Trotsky defended the use of violence as a necessary tool of revolution, and they frequently pointed to the 25 million casualties from the recent slaughter of World War I to justify the violence practiced by the Bolshevik government.

The civil war exacted its toll on Russia and on Lenin. By the time of the final Bolshevik victory in 1921, the country lay in absolute ruin. The economy, which collapsed at the outset of the Russian war, was virtually destroyed. Lenin, in an effort to begin the rebuilding of the economy, issued a decree ending the draconian laws of War Communism. In its place, he instituted the New Economic Policy, which

(continued on the next page)

LENIN (LEFT) IS PICTURED HERE WITH JOSEPH STALIN IN AUGUST 1922. BEFORE HIS DEATH IN 1924, LENIN EXPRESSED IN HIS FINAL POLITICAL "TESTAMENT" THAT HE HAD A GREAT FEAR FOR THE STABILITY OF THE PARTY UNDER THE LEASERSHIP OF THE FORECFUL PERSONALITIES OF STALIN AND TROTSKY.

(continued from the previous page)

allowed for a modest resumption of capitalist relations. Restrictions on opposition newspapers were gradually reduced, though never repealed, and the Bolshevik government brought an end to the indiscriminate use of terror that had characterized the civil war period. In one respect, however, Lenin tightened the control of the government, as he decreed that the Bolshevik Party would tolerate no dissension in its ranks, and he outlawed the forming of factions within the party.

Lenin's actions during the last years of his life provided much grist for the mill of his successors and for historians, who have often questioned what course the Soviet Union would have pursued had Lenin's failing health not shortened his life. Some have suggested that Lenin would have continued with the policies that he introduced in 1921, hoping to bring the Soviet Union modestly along the course to socialism. The actual course pursued by Lenin's eventual successor, Joseph Stalin, was clearly of the other extreme. Stalin would restore the most draconian of Lenin's policies, reintroducing the terror, the radical economic policies, and the overall concept of forcing revolution with cold-blooded determination that far surpassed Lenin in ruthlessness. The instruments that Stalin used to carry out his radical policies—from the centralized party to the fierce secret police—had all been established during Lenin's reign. Knowledge of the course that Lenin intended to take, however, went with him to his grave. Lenin suffered two strokes in 1922 and a third in 1923 that severely impaired his ability to function. A final stroke on January 21, 1924, in the village of Gorki (now Gorki Leninskiye), near Moscow, ended his life.

During the Soviet era, Lenin was hailed as the greatest national hero of the country. His writings—particularly his directives for the Communist Party—ranked with those of Marx. Lenin's tomb, in Red Square in Moscow, was a national shrine. In 1924 Petrograd was renamed Leningrad in his honor. After the demise of communism and the breakup of the Soviet Union in 1991, however, the Russian

(continued on the next page)

(continued from the previous page)

people began to turn against Lenin and all he stood for. The citizens of Leningrad in 1991 voted to restore the city's name to St. Petersburg. The fierce attachment—both in support and in disdain—that the Russian population continued to feel toward Lenin would be seen even in the waning days of the century that he had influenced so fundamentally, as the Russian Parliament staged fierce debates over whether Lenin's body should be exhumed from his tomb in Moscow or left as a shrine to the Soviet period.

WAR COMMUNISM

Lenin did not favour moving toward a socialist economy after October, because the Bolsheviks lacked the necessary economic skills. He preferred state capitalism, with capitalist managers staying in place but supervised by the workforce. Others, like Bukharin, wanted a rapid transition to a socialist economy. The civil war caused the Bolsheviks to adopt a more severe economic policy known as War Communism, characterized chiefly by the expropriation of private business and industry and the forced requisition of grain and other food products from the peasants. The Bolsheviks subsequently clashed with the labour force, which understood socialism as industrial self-management. Ever-present hunger exacerbated the poor labour relations, and strikes became endemic, especially in Petrograd. The Bolsheviks, however, pressed ahead, using coercion as necessary. The story was the same in the countryside. Food had to be requisitioned in order to feed the cities and the Red Army. The Reds informed the peasants that it was in their best interests to supply food, because if the landlords came back the peasants would lose everything.

These measures negatively affected both agricultural and industrial production. With no incentives to grow surplus grain (since it would just be confiscated), the peasants' production of it and other crops plummeted, with the result that starvation came to threaten many city dwellers. In the cities, a large and untrained bureaucracy was hastily created to supervise the newly centralized, state-owned economy, with the result that labour productivity and industrial output plummeted. By 1921 industrial production had dropped to one-fifth of its prewar levels (that is to say, in 1913), and the real wages of urban workers had declined by an estimated two-thirds in just three years. Uncontrolled inflation rendered paper currency worthless, and so the government had to resort to the exchange and distribution of goods and services without the use of money.

Soviet Russia adopted its first constitution in July 1918 and fashioned treaties with other republics such as Ukraine. The latter was vital for the economic viability of Russia, and Bolshevik will was imposed. It was also imposed in the Caucasus, where Georgia, Armenia, and Azerbaijan were tied to Bolshevik Russia by 1921. Many Communists regarded Russia as acquiring imperialist ambitions. Indeed, Moscow under the Georgian Joseph Stalin, the commissar for nationalities, regarded imperial Russia's territory as its natural patrimony. Russia lost control of the Baltic states and Finland, however. Lenin's nationality policy was based on the assumption that nations would choose to stay in a close relationship with Russia, but this proved not to be the case. Many republics wanted to be independent to develop their own brand of national communism. The comrade who imposed Russian dominance was, ironically, Stalin. As commissar for nationalities, he sought to ensure that Moscow rule prevailed.

By early 1921 public discontent with the state of the economy had spread from the countryside to the cities, resulting in numerous strikes and protests that culminated in March of that year in the Kronshtadt Rebellion.

KRONSHTADT REBELLION

The Kronshtadt, also spelled Kronštadt, Rebellion (March 1921) was one of several major internal uprisings against Soviet rule in Russia after the civil war (1918–20) and was conducted by sailors from the Kronshtadt naval base. It greatly influenced the Communist Party's decision to undertake a program of economic liberalization to relieve the hardships suffered by the Russian population during the civil war.

The sailors, located at the Kronshtadt fortress in the Gulf of Finland overlooking Petrograd, had supported the Bolsheviks in 1917; their cooperation had been crucial to the success of the October Revolution. During the civil war, however, they had become disenchanted with the Bolshevik government, which had been unable to provide an adequate food supply to urban populations and had restricted their political freedoms and imposed harsh labour regulations.

When the urban workers responded (early 1921) with strikes and demonstrations, the Kronshtadt sailors, sympathizing with them, formed a Provisional Revolutionary Committee. In addition to economic reform, they demanded "soviets without Bolsheviks," the release of non-Bolshevik socialists from prison, the end of the Communist Party's dictatorship, and the establishment of political freedoms and civil rights.

THE KRONSHTADT REBELLION, AN UNSUCCESSFUL UPRISING BY SAILORS, SOLDIERS, AND CIVILIANS AGAINST THE BOLSHEVIKS IN MARCH 1921, PROMPTED LENIN TO RELAX CONTROLS OVER THE RUSSIAN ECONOMY TO HELP RELIEVE THE HARDSHIPS SUFFERED BY THE RUSSIANS DURING THE CIVIL WAR.

Leon Trotsky and Mikhail N. Tukhachevsky led a force that crushed the rebels, shooting or imprisoning the survivors. Nevertheless, by dramatically demonstrating popular dissatisfaction with the Communists' policies, the rebellion forced the party to adopt the New Economic Policy (March 1921), which brought economic relief to Soviet Russia, but made them temporarily abandon their attempts to achieve a socialist economic system by government decree.

THE NEW ECONOMIC POLICY AND COLLECTIVISM

F orced requisitioning led to peasant revolts, and the Tambov province revolt of 1920 in particular forced Lenin to change his War Communism policy. He and the Bolshevik leadership were willing to slaughter the mutinous sailors of the Kronshtadt naval base in March 1921, but they could not survive if the countryside turned against them. They would simply starve to death. A tactical retreat from enforced socialism was deemed necessary, a move that was deeply unpopular with the Bolshevik rank and file.

THE NEP

The New Economic Policy (NEP) was inaugurated at the 10th Party Congress in March 1921. These measures included the

МЕШОЧНИК–ВРАГ ТРАНСПОРТА,–ВРАГ–РЕСПУБЛИКИ.

THIS LITHOGRAPH FROM 1921 EXPLAINS THAT THE MIDDLE MAN IS THE ENEMY OF TRANSPORT AND THE ENEMY OF THE REPUBLIC. IN THE NEW ECONOMIC POLICY, THE STATE KEPT CONTROL OF TRANSPORTATION, LARGE-SCALE INDUSTRY, COMMUNICATIONS, BANKING, AND TRADE WITH OTHER COUNTRIES. MUCH OF THE AGRICULTURE, RETAIL TRADE, AND SMALL INDUSTRIES RETURNED TO PRIVATE OWNERS.

return of most agriculture, retail trade, and small-scale light industry to private ownership and management while the state retained control of heavy industry, transport, communications, banking, and foreign trade. Money was reintroduced into the economy in 1922 (it had been abolished under War Communism). The peasants were allowed to own and cultivate their own land, while paying taxes to the state. The New Economic Policy reintroduced a measure of stability to the economy and allowed the Soviet people to recover from years of war, civil war, and governmental mismanagement. The small businessmen and managers who flourished in this period became known as NEP men. The economy was back to its 1913 level by the mid-1920s, and this permitted a vigorous debate on the future. All Communist Party members agreed that the goal was socialism, and this meant the dominance of the industrial economy. The working class, the natural constituency of the Communist Party, had to grow rapidly. There was also the question of the country's security. Moscow lived in fear of an attack during the 1920s and concluded a number of peace treaties and nonaggression pacts with neighbouring and other countries.

LENINISM

The principles expounded by Vladimir I. Lenin are called Leninism (also referred to as Bolshevism or Marxism-Leninism). Whether Leninist concepts represented a contribution to or a corruption of Marxist thought has been debated, but their influence on the subsequent development of communism in the Soviet Union and elsewhere has been of fundamental importance.

In the *Communist Manifesto* (1848), Karl Marx and Friedrich Engels defined Communists as "the most advanced and resolute section of the working-class parties of every country, that section which pushes forward all others." This conception was fundamental to Leninist thought. Lenin saw the Communist Party as a highly committed intellectual elite who (1) had a scientific understanding of history and society in the light of Marxist principles, (2) were committed to ending capitalism and instituting socialism in its place, (3) were bent on forcing through this transition after having achieved political power, and (4) were committed to attaining this power by any means possible, including violence and revolution if necessary. Lenin's emphasis upon action by a small, deeply committed group stemmed both from the need for efficiency and discretion in the revolutionary movement and from an authoritarian bent that was present in all of his political thought. The authoritarian aspect of Leninism appeared also in its insistence upon the need for a "proletarian dictatorship" following the seizure of power, a dictatorship that in practice was exercised not by the workers but by the leaders of the Communist Party.

At the root of Leninist authoritarianism was a distrust of spontaneity, a conviction that historical events, if left to themselves, would not bring the desired outcome—i.e., the coming into being of a socialist society. Lenin was not at all convinced, for instance, that the workers would inevitably acquire the proper revolutionary and class consciousness of the Communist elite; he was instead afraid that they would be content with the gains in living and working conditions obtained through trade-union activity. In this, Leninism differed from traditional Marxism, which predicted that material conditions would suffice to make workers conscious of the need for revolution. For Lenin, then, the Communist elite—the "workers' vanguard"—was more than a catalytic agent that precipitated events along their inevitable course; it was an indispensable element.

Just as Leninism was pragmatic in its choice of means to achieve political power, it was also opportunistic in the policies it adopted and the compromises it made to maintain its hold on power. A good example of this is Lenin's own New Economic Policy (1921–28), which temporarily restored the market economy and some private enterprise in the Soviet Union after the disastrous economic results of War Communism (1918–21).

In practice, Leninism's unrestrained pursuit of a socialist society resulted in the creation of a totalitarian state in the Soviet Union. If the conditions of Russia in its backward state of development did not lead to socialism naturally, then, after coming to power, the Bolsheviks would legislate socialism into existence and

(continued on the next page)

A TRIAL OF THE LEADERS OF THE SOCIALIST-REVOLUTIONARY PARTY TAKES PLACE IN MOSCOW IN AUGUST 1922. LENIN INSTRUCTED SUCH "SHOW TRIALS" TO TAKE PLACE TO TERRORIZE AND SUPPRESS LEFT-WING ORGANIZATIONS THAT OPPOSED THE BOL-SHEVIKS. THE USE OF SHOW TRIALS ESCALATED DURING STALIN'S DICTATORSHIP.

(continued from the previous page)

would exercise despotic control to break public resistance. Thus, every aspect of the Soviet Union's political, economic, cultural, and intellectual life came to be regulated by the Communist Party in a strict and regimented fashion that would tolerate no opposition. The building of the socialist society proceeded under a new autocracy of Communist Party officials and bureaucrats. Marxism and Leninism originally expected that, with the triumph of the proletariat, the state that Marx had defined as the organ of class rule would "wither away" because class conflicts would come to an end. Communist rule in the Soviet Union resulted instead in the vastly increased power of the state apparatus. Terror was applied without hesitation, humanitarian considerations and individual rights were disregarded, and the assumption of the class character of all intellectual and moral life led to a relativization of the standards of truth, ethics, and justice. Leninism thus created the first modern totalitarian state.

THE UNION OF SOVIET SOCIALIST REPUBLICS

Soviet Russia gave way to the Union of Soviet Socialist Republics (U.S.S.R.) in 1922, but this did not mean that Russia gave up its hegemony within the new state. As before, Moscow was the capital, and it dominated the union. Lenin's death in January 1924 set off a succession struggle that lasted until the end of the decade. Stalin eventually outwitted Trotsky, Lenin's natural successor, and various other contenders. Stalin, who had become general secretary of the party in 1922, used the party as a power base. The economic debate was won by those who favoured rapid industrialization and forced collectivization. The NEP engendered not only a flowering of Russian culture but also that of non-Russian and non-Slavic cultures. Russia itself had been an empire with many non-Russian citizens, and the emergence of numerous national elites was a trend of considerable concern to Stalin and his leadership.

ARTIST IVAN SILYCH GORYSHKIN-SKOROPUDOV DEPICTED LENIN'S FUNERAL CEREMONY IN 1924 WITH MOURNER AND HEIR-APPARENT JOSEPH STALIN STANDING BEHIND LENIN. STALIN OUT-MANEUVERED HIS RIVAL TROTSKY FOR LEADERSHIP AND EVEN MISLEAD TROTSKY ABOUT THE DETAILS OF LENIN'S FUNERAL SO TROTSKY WAS UNABLE TO ATTEND.

But the NEP was viewed by the Soviet government as merely a temporary expedient to allow the economy to recover while the Communists solidified their hold on power. By 1925 Nikolay Bukharin had become the foremost supporter of the NEP, while Leon Trotsky was opposed to it and Joseph Stalin was noncommittal. The NEP was dogged by the government's chronic inability to procure enough grain supplies from the peasantry to feed its urban workforce. (In 1928–29 these grain shortages prompted Joseph Stalin, by then the country's paramount leader, to forcibly eliminate the private ownership of farmland and to collectivize agriculture under the state's control, thus ensuring the procurement of adequate food supplies for the cities in the future. This abrupt policy change, which was accompanied by the destruction of several million of the country's most prosperous private farmers, marked the end of the NEP. It was followed by the reimposition of state control over all industry and commerce in the country by 1931.)

NIKOLAY IVANOVICH BUKHARIN

Born on October 9 [Sept. 27, Old Style], 1888, in Moscow, Nikolay Ivanovich Bukharin was a Bolshevik and Marxist theoretician and economist and a prominent leader of the Communist International (Comintern). Bukharin died on March 14, 1938, in Moscow).

Having become a revolutionary while studying economics, Bukharin joined the Russian Social-Democratic Workers' Party in 1906 and became a member of the Moscow committee of the party's Bolshevik wing in 1908. He was arrested and deported to Onega (a region near the White Sea) in 1911 but escaped to western Europe, where he met the Bolshevik leader Lenin in Kraków (1912) and worked with him on the party's newspaper *Pravda* ("Truth"). In October 1916 he went to New York, where he edited a Leninist newspaper, *Novy Mir* ("New World").

After the February Revolution of 1917, Bukharin returned to Russia. He was elected to his party's central committee in August, and, after the Bolsheviks seized power, he became editor of *Pravda*. In 1918, when Lenin insisted upon signing the Brest-Litovsk treaty with Germany and withdrawing Russia from World War I, Bukharin briefly resigned his post at *Pravda* and led an opposition group, the Left Communists, which proposed instead to transform the war into a general Communist revolution throughout Europe. In March 1919 he became a member of the Comintern's executive committee. During the next few years he published several theoretical economic works, including *The Economics of the Transitional Period* (1920), *The ABC of Communism* (with Yevgeny Preobrazhensky; 1921), and *The Theory of Historical Materialism* (1921).

After Lenin's death in 1924, Bukharin became a full member of the Politburo. He continued to be a principal supporter of Lenin's New Economic Policy (promulgated in 1921), which promoted gradual economic change, and opposed the policy of initiating rapid industrialization and collectivization in agriculture. For a time Bukharin was thus allied with Stalin, who used this issue to undermine his chief rivals—Leon Trotsky, Grigory Zinovyev, and Lev Kamenev. In 1926 Bukharin succeeded Zinovyev as chairman of the Comintern's executive committee. Nevertheless, in 1928 Stalin reversed himself, espoused the program of enforced collectivization advocated by his defeated opponents, and denounced Bukharin for opposing it. Bukharin lost his Comintern post in April 1929 and was expelled from the Politburo in November. He recanted his views under pressure and was partially reinstated in the party by Stalin. But though he was made editor of *Izvestia*, the official government newspaper, in 1934 and participated in writing the 1936 Soviet constitution, he never regained his earlier influence and power. Bukharin was secretly arrested in January 1937 and was expelled from the Communist Party for being a "Trotskyite." In March 1938 he was a defendant in the last public purge trial, falsely accused of counterrevolutionary activities and of espionage, found guilty, and executed. He was posthumously reinstated as a party member in 1988.

JOSEPH STALIN BECOMES SUPREME RULER

During the civil war in 1918–20 following the revolution, Stalin served as political commissar with Bolshevik armies on several fronts. At that time political commissars were entrusted with military duties, and Stalin showed exceptional ability as a strategist and tactician. In 1918 he directed the successful defense of the vital city of Tsaritsyn against the White Army. Tsaritsyn was

FOUR BOLSHEVIK LEADERS OF THE OLD GUARD ARE SEEN HERE WALKING TO A MEETING OF THE CENTRAL EXECUTIVE COMMITTEE OF THE COMMUNIST PARTY IN JUNE 1925. FROM THE LEFT ARE JOSEPH STALIN, ALEKSEY RYKOV, LEV KAMENEV, AND GRIGORY ZINOVYEV. STALIN TURNED ON THE OTHERS AND EVENTUALLY BECAME SUPREME RULER.

renamed Stalingrad in his honor in 1925, though the name was later changed to Volgograd as part of an effort in the 1950s and '60s to downgrade Stalin's importance. In 1921 Stalin led the invasion that won his homeland, Georgia, for the Communists, as the Bolsheviks now called themselves. The next year Stalin became Secretary General of the Central Committee of the Communist Party, and he methodically assumed increasing power.

Some of Stalin's unscrupulous methods worried even Lenin, who wrote, "Stalin is too rough." Stalin, however, was undisturbed by criticism. Grimly he undermined his rival Leon Trotsky, the Soviet Union's war minister and Lenin's former close associate.

Ruthless and cunning, Stalin—born Iosif Djugashvili—seemed intent on living up to his revolutionary surname (which means "man of steel"). In 1925, a year after Lenin's death, Stalin forced Trotsky to resign as war minister and in 1927 expelled him from the party. Determined to eliminate the minority Trotskyite influence, Stalin exiled Trotsky from the Soviet Union in 1929 and had him assassinated in Mexico in 1940. Having dealt with the opposition, Stalin was then supreme ruler.

STALIN'S FIVE-YEAR PLANS

In a drive to industrialize and modernize the Soviet Union, Stalin launched the first in a series of five-year plans in 1928. The first Five-Year Plan (1928–32) concentrated on developing heavy industry and collectivizing agriculture, at the cost of a drastic fall in consumer goods. Stalin ordered the collectivization of farms. When peasants resisted, he ordered the state to seize their land and possessions. Well-to-do farmers, called kulaks, especially resented collectivization. Determined to root out all opposition, Stalin showed no mercy to the rebellious kulaks, and thousands were shot, exiled, or placed in concentration camps and worked to death under atrocious conditions.

The second plan (1933–37) continued the objectives of the first. Collectivization led to terrible famines, especially in Ukraine, that caused the deaths of millions. The third (1938–42) emphasized the production of armaments and

К КОНЦУ ПЯТИЛЕТКИ
КОЛЛЕКТИВИЗАЦИЯ СССР ДОЛЖНА
БЫТЬ В ОСНОВНОМ ЗАКОНЧЕНА"
(И. СТАЛИН)

"..РАБОЧИЙ КЛАСС СОВЕТСКОГО
СОЮЗА ТВЕРДО И УВЕРЕННО
ВЕДЕТ ВПЕРЕД ДЕЛО ТЕХНИЧЕСКОГО
ПЕРЕВООРУЖЕНИЯ СВОЕГО СОЮЗНИКА-
ТРУДОВОГО КРЕСТЬЯНСТВА"
(И. СТАЛИН)

ARTIST GUSTAVE KLUTSIS MADE THIS POSTER PROMOTING STALIN'S FIRST FIVE-YEAR PLAN AND ANNOUNCING THAT BY THE END OF IT COLLECTIVIZATION SHOULD BE COMPLETED.

was suspended by the invasion of Germany in World War II. The fourth (1946–53) again stressed heavy industry and military buildup, angering the Western powers. Stalin proceeded to carry out additional Five-Year plans in the years after World War II, in keeping with his promise to make the Soviet Union the top industrial nation by 1960.

COLLECTIVIZATION

The Soviet government pursued most intensively collectivization between 1929 and 1933, to transform traditional agriculture in the Soviet Union and to reduce the economic power of the kulaks. Under collectivization the peasants were forced to give up their individual farms and join large collective farms, called kolkhozy. The process was ultimately undertaken in conjunction with the campaign to industrialize the Soviet Union rapidly. But before the drive began, long and bitter debates over the nature and pace of collectivization went on among the Soviet leaders (especially between Stalin and Trotsky, 1925–27, and between Stalin and Nikolay Bukharin, 1927–29).

Some Soviet leaders considered collective farms a socialist form of land tenure and therefore desirable; but they advocated a gradual transition to them to avoid disrupting the agricultural productivity necessary to stimulate industrial growth. Other leaders favoured rapid industrialization and, consequently, wanted immediate, forced collectivization; they argued not only that the large kolkhozy could use heavy machinery more efficiently and produce larger crops than could numerous small, individual farms but that they

Labourers meet to discuss harvesting on a collective farm in Kiev, Ukraine, between 1930 and 1940. By 1930 more than one-half of the peasant farmers had been compelled to be part of a collective farm.

could be controlled more effectively by the state. As a result, they could be forced to sell a large proportion of their output to the state at low government prices, thereby enabling the state to acquire the capital necessary for the development of heavy industry.

A decision was made by the 15th Congress of the Communist Party (December 1927) to undertake collectivization at a gradual pace, allowing the peasantry to join kolkhozy voluntarily. But in November 1928 the Central Committee (and in April 1929 the 16th Party Conference) approved plans that increased the goals and called for 20 percent of the nation's farmland to be collectivized by 1933. Between October 1929 and January 1930 the proportion of peasant households forced into kolkhozy rose from about 4 percent to 21 percent, although the government's main efforts in the countryside were concentrated on extracting grain from the kulaks.

Intensive collectivization began during the winter of 1929–30. Stalin called upon the party to "liquidate the kulaks as a class" (December 27, 1929), and the Central Committee resolved that an "enormous majority" of the peasant households should be collectivized by 1933. Harsh measures—including land confiscations, arrests, and deportations to prison camps—were inflicted upon all peasants who resisted collectivization. By March 1930 more than one-half of the peasantry (a larger proportion in the agriculturally rich southwestern region of the Soviet Union) had been forced to join collective farms.

CONCLUSION

Nicholas II, son of Alexander III, came to power in 1894. Weak willed and indecisive, he was unsuited for the task of ruling a vast empire. In 1904 Russia and Japan went to war over Russia's expansionist activities in the Far East. The war was unpopular in Russia, and the country suffered a terrible defeat, encouraging greater revolutionary activity.

Although small, a new factory laboring class was organized by the revolutionaries. Peasants sympathized and helped. Mutinies broke out in the army and navy. Manufacturers and landlords demanded reforms that would satisfy workers, peasants, and soldiers. The Revolution of 1905 reached its climax with a general strike and the formation of a soviet, or workers' council, in St. Petersburg. In response, Nicholas called for the election of a duma as proposed by his ancestor Alexander I a century before.

In August 1914 Russia went to war against Germany and Austria over conflicting claims in the Balkans. The peasants and workers at first accepted the war without protest, but great military failures resulted because of the Russian government's inability to equip its armies. Millions of Russian lives were sacrificed. The attitude of the public toward the war and the government changed.

Food shortages in early 1917 sparked mass rioting in the capital of Petrograd (formerly St. Petersburg). Soldiers deserted the government and joined the people. The Duma demanded that the tsar step down. Nicholas II abdicated his throne on March 15, ending more than 300 years of rule by the Romanov Dynasty. He and his family were exiled to Siberia and later executed.

In the second phase of the Russian Revolution, in October 1917, a group of radical socialists called the Bolsheviks, under the leadership of Lenin, emerged as the preeminent power in Russia. In 1918 they changed their name to the Russian Communist Party. Between 1918 and 1920 the Red Army successfully defended the new government against anticommunist forces in a civil war. In 1921 Lenin inaugurated the New Economic Policy (NEP), encouraging individual initiative in the farm sector. The NEP temporarily reinvigorated the Soviet economy by providing sufficient food for everyone.

The Communist government officially established the Union of Soviet Socialist Republics (U.S.S.R.) on December 30, 1922. The U.S.S.R. was composed of Russia, Belorussia (now Belarus), Ukraine, and the Transcaucasian Federation. The first constitution was formally adopted in January 1924. In February 1924, Great Britain's government officially recognized the U.S.S.R., and soon other nations did as well. In 1925 the All-Union Communist Party, later the Communist Party of the Soviet Union, was formed. The Russian Soviet Federated Socialist Republic dominated the Soviet Union for its entire

74-year history. It was by far the largest of the republics, and Moscow, its capital, was also the capital of the Soviet Union.

The Soviet Union was the first country in the world to adopt a Communist government based on Marxism, the theories of the German revolutionary Karl Marx. In a Communist society, the major means of economic production, such as farms, factories, and mines, are owned by the public or the government, not individuals. Wealth is divided among all people either equally or according to their needs. Lenin, the principal architect of the Soviet Union and its first leader, adapted Marxism to Russian conditions. His version of Communism came to be called Marxism-Leninism. The Soviet government took control of nearly all the land and industries in the country, and the Soviet Communist party came to dominate all aspects of the country's political, economic, social, and cultural life. As a collectivist society, it was based on the principle that the welfare of the collective—meaning all of society—is more important than individual liberties.

Lenin died in 1924, and a struggle for leadership began between Joseph Stalin and Leon Trotsky. As secretary of the Central Committee of the Communist Party, Stalin stripped Trotsky of power and exiled him in 1928.

Stalin continued Lenin's NEP until 1928. Fearing the entrenchment of a capitalist class in agriculture, however, he initiated the first Five-Year Plan. The plan called for rapid growth in heavy industry and collectivization of agriculture.

Rapid and forced collectivization of agriculture resulted in great inefficiencies, the deportation of millions of the wealthier peasants, and confiscation of grain. Rather than yield their livestock to the new collectives, many farmers slaughtered them. A man-made famine resulted. In 1932 about three million people died of starvation in Ukraine

Factory workers assemble tractors on a line in Russia in 1930. Stalin ruthlessly pushed for rapid growth in heavy industry and collectivization in agriculture to make the Soviet Union a dominant power on the world stage.

alone. Nevertheless, when the first Five-Year Plan ended in 1932, the government announced that great progress had been made. Peasant resistance had been smashed, and the country was on the road to industrialization.

Stalin meanwhile tightened his grip on the government and the Red Army by means of a series of purges. In 1935 and 1936 nearly 500,000 people were executed, imprisoned, or forced into labor camps. He further consolidated his position through the Great Purge trials of 1936–39. Through this system Stalin eliminated his rivals. He systematically employed the services of the secret police (later known as the KGB) to root out "political criminals."

Stalin's foreign policy was equally ruthless. Like Lenin, he believed that the Soviet state would never be totally secure until the entire world was Communist. Many nations were disturbed by the Third, or Communist, International, known as the Comintern. The Comintern directed the activities of Communist parties outside the Soviet Union. It gathered information by espionage, caused labor troubles and other civil discord, and undermined governments.

Beginning as an impoverished country, the Soviet Union made great strides in industrializing and improving its economy. Marxism-Leninism, as an alternative to capitalism, thus appealed to leaders of some developing countries—nations where there were many dispossessed and impoverished people and where a few people had most of the wealth. The Soviet constitution openly supported "wars of liberation" wherever and whenever they occurred. After World War II the country helped to install Communist governments in most of Eastern Europe, and the Soviet Union and United States (and their respective allies) opposed each other in a long, hostile rivalry called the Cold War. Whether Western countries viewed the Soviet Union as a powerful rival or a threat, it could not be ignored.

In the 1980s the Soviet Union began to change. Following decades of political and cultural repression and bureaucratic and economic stagnation, the Soviet government after 1984 was given an injection of fresh, new leadership. General Secretary Mikhail Gorbachev introduced a vast array of perestroika (restructuring), or reform of political and economic policy. He also instituted the liberal policy of glasnost (openness), which allowed political and social issues to be discussed openly. A host of peace proposals was proffered, resulting in a major nuclear arms reduction agreement with the United States. In less than a decade, however, these policies led to the dissolution of the Soviet Union in 1991.

GLOSSARY

ABDICATION The process of giving up sovereign power, office, or responsibility, usually formally; renouncement.

ABROGATE To do away with or cancel by authoritative action.

ANNUL To make ineffective or inoperative; to declare or make legally void.

AUTOCRACY Government in which one person possesses unlimited power.

BOLSHEVIK A member of the radical wing of the Russian Social Democratic Party, which seized power in Russia by the revolution of November 1917.

BYNAME A secondary name; a nickname.

CHEKA The early Soviet secret police agency and a forerunner of the KGB.

COMMISSAR The head of a government department in the Soviet Union from 1917 to 1946.

COMMUNE A rural community, such as the Russian mir, that is organized on a communal basis.

COMPULSORY Required by authority.

CONSTITUTIONAL MONARCHY A system of government in which a monarch shares power with a constitutionally organized government.

DEPRECATE To express disapproval of.

DISSIDENT One who openly differs with an opinion or a group.

DUMA The principal legislative assembly in Russia from 1906 to 1917 and since 1993.

EXPROPRIATION The act of taking away from a person the possession of or right to property.

KOLKHOZ (PLURAL, KOLKHOZY) A collective farm of the Soviet Union.

KULAK A prosperous or wealthy peasant farmer in early 20th century Russia.

MANIFESTO A public declaration of policy, purpose, or views.

MENSHEVIK A member of a wing of the Russian Social Democratic party before and during the Russian Revolution believing in the gradual achievement of socialism by parliamentary methods in opposition to the Bolsheviks.

POGROM An organized slaughter of helpless people and especially of Jews.

PROBITY Adherence to the highest principles and ideals; uprightness.

PROMULGATE To put (a law) into action or force.

PROPAGANDA The spreading of ideas, information, or rumor for the purpose of helping or injuring a cause.

RUSSIFICATION The act or process of being Russianized; the act of bringing a region or national group under the national control of Russia; forcing someone to conform to a Russian cultural pattern or political organization.

SOVIET An elected governmental council in a Communist country; Bolshevik; the people and especially the political and military leaders of the Union of Soviet Socialist Republics.

TOTALITARIAN Of or relating to, or being a political regime based on subordination of the individual to the state and strict control of all aspects of life especially by use of force.

ZEMSTVO One of the district and provincial assemblies established in Russia in 1864.

BIBLIOGRAPHY

ON RUSSIAN HISTORY

Glenn E. Curtis, *Russia: A Country Study* (1998). Denis J. B. Shaw, *Russia in the Modern World: A New Geography* (1999), examines the spatial structures of Russia, including those of polity, culture, economy, and rural and urban life, with a descriptive discussion of the country's traditional 11 economic regions.

Russia from 1801 to 1904: General surveys of Russian history in the 19th century include David Saunders, *Russia in the Age of Reaction and Reform, 1801–1881* (1992); and Hugh Seton-Watson, *The Russian Empire, 1801–1917* (1967, reprinted 1990). An excellent English-language work on the reign of Alexander I is Janet M. Hartley, *Alexander I* (1994). Politics during the reign of Alexander I is discussed in Alexander M. Martin, *Romantics, Reformers, and Reactionaries: Russian Conservative Thought and Politics in the Reign of Alexander I* (1997). The reign of Nicholas I is explored in W. Bruce Lincoln, *Nicholas I, Emperor and Autocrat of All the Russias* (1978, reprinted 1989). The general economic development of Russia in the 19th century is analyzed in W. Bruce Lincoln, *The Great Reforms: Autocracy, Bureaucracy, and the Politics of Change in Imperial Russia* (1990); Ben Eklof, John Bushnell, and Larissa Zakharova (eds.), *Russia's Great Reforms, 1855–1881* (1994); and Arcadius Kahan, *Russian Economic History: The Nineteenth Century*, ed. by Roger Weiss (1989). An analysis of reform and counterreform dynamics is given in Thomas S. Pearson, *Russian Officialdom in Crisis: Autocracy and Local Self-Government, 1861–1900* (1989, reissued 2002). Dominic Lieven, *Nicholas II* (1993, reissued 1996), examines the personality of Nicholas II and his reign. Studies of important issues in Russian foreign policy and the emergence of the Russian Empire include William C. Fuller, Jr., *Strat-*

egy and Power in Russia, 1600–1914 (1992); Dietrich Geyer, *Russian Imperialism: The Interaction of Domestic and Foreign Policy, 1860–1914*, trans. by Bruce Little (1987; originally published in German, 1977); Andreas Kappeler, *The Russian Empire: A Multiethnic History*, trans. by Alfred Clayton (2001; originally published in German, 1992); Dominic Lieven, *Empire: The Russian Empire and Its Rivals* (2000, reissued 2003); and Geoffrey Hosking, *Russia: People and Empire, 1552–1917* (1997).

Russia from 1905 to 1917: An excellent general introduction to the period is Hans Rogger, *Russia in the Age of Modernisation and Revolution, 1881–1917* (1983). Foreign policy is the subject of Barbara Jelavich, *Russia's Balkan Entanglements, 1806–1914* (1991, reissued 2002); David MacLaren McDonald, *United Government and Foreign Policy in Russia, 1900–1914* (1992); and Dominic Lieven, *Russia and the Origins of the First World War* (1983). Dominic Lieven, *Russia's Rulers Under the Old Regime* (1989), offers a collective portrait of the policy makers. The economy of the period is examined in Peter Gatrell, *The Tsarist Economy, 1850–1917* (1986). The Revolution of 1905 is addressed in Abraham Ascher, *The Revolution of 1905*, 2 vol. (1988–92); and Andrew M. Verner, *The Crisis of Russian Autocracy: Nicholas II and the 1905 Revolution* (1990). A more comparative socioeconomic approach to the revolution is demonstrated in Teodor Shanin, *The Roots of Otherness: Russia's Turn of Century*, 2 vol. (1986), which concentrates especially on the peasantry. The reaction of the elites to the revolution is analyzed in Roberta Thompson Manning, *The Crisis of the Old Order in Russia: Gentry and Government* (1982). The politics of the new parliament, the Duma, is outlined in Geoffrey A. Hosking, *The Russian Constitutional Experiment: Government and Duma, 1907–1914* (1973); and the social dimension of the new politics is examined in Leopold H. Haimson (ed.), *The Politics of Rural Russia, 1905–1914* (1979); and Victoria E. Bonnell,

Roots of Rebellion: Workers' Politics and Organizations in St. Petersburg and Moscow, 1900–1914 (1983). Russia's problems during World War I are described in Michael T. Florinsky, *The End of the Russian Empire* (1931, reprinted 1973). The revolutionary period is the subject of Orlando Figes, *A People's Tragedy* (1996, reissued 1998).

Soviet Russia: For the Soviet period there are hardly any specific histories of Russia, which is always treated in the wider context of the Soviet Union. An overview of the Revolution of 1917 and its consequences is offered in Sheila Fitzpatrick, *The Russian Revolution*, 2nd ed. (1994, reissued 2001). Robert Service, *A History of Twentieth-Century Russia* (1998), is an excellent one-volume history of the Soviet state. Christopher Read, *The Making and Breaking of the Soviet System* (2001), provides a stimulating analysis of the causes of the rise and fall of the Soviet Union. Relevant historical biographies include Robert Service, *Lenin: A Biography* (2000); Robert C. Tucker, *Stalin as Revolutionary, 1879–1929* (1973), and *Stalin in Power, 1928–1941* (1990); and William J. Tompson, *Khrushchev: A Political Life* (1995, reissued 1997). Chris Ward (ed.), *The Stalinist Dictatorship* (1998), is a readable examination of the Stalinist period. The Gorbachev era is analyzed in Archie Brown, *The Gorbachev Factor* (1996); Stephen White, *After Gorbachev*, 4th ed. (1994), a solid narrative of the years of perestroika; Richard Sakwa, *Gorbachev and His Reforms, 1985–1990* (1990); Jeffrey F. Hough, *Democratization and Revolution in the USSR, 1985–1991* (1997); and Mikhail Gorbachev, *Perestroika: New Thinking for Our Country and the World*, new, updated ed. (1988), and *Memoirs* (1996), which reveals insights into Gorbachev's thinking. Good introductions to the Soviet political structure and situation are Richard Sakwa, *Soviet Politics in Perspective*, 2nd ed. rev. (1998); Gordon B. Smith, *Soviet Politics: Struggling with Change*, 2nd ed. (1992); Geoffrey Ponton, *The Soviet Era: Soviet Politics from Lenin to Yeltsin* (1994); and Evan Mawdsley and Stephen White, *The Soviet Elite from Lenin* to Gorbachev: *The Central Committee and Its Members, 1917–1991* (2000), a wide-ranging survey. Alec Nove, *An Economic History of the USSR, 1917–1991*, 3rd ed. (1992), is an informed, accessible account. The breakup of the Soviet Union is the subject of Ronald Grigor Suny, *The Revenge of the Past: Nationalism, Revolution, and the Collapse of the Soviet Union* (1993); and Roman Szporluk, *Russia, Ukraine, and the Breakup of the Soviet Union* (2000). Foreign policy is discussed in Gabriel Gorodetsky (ed.), *Soviet Foreign Policy, 1917–1991: A Retrospective* (1994). Vladislav Zubok and Constantine Pleshakov, *Inside the Kremlin's Cold War: From Stalin to Khrushchev* (1996), uses archival material released in the 1990s to examine the Cold War and its origins from the Soviet point of view. The secret police's role during the Soviet period is the subject of Amy W. Knight, *The KGB: Police and Politics in the Soviet Union*, rev. ed. (1990).

ON NICHOLAS II

Dominic Lieven, *Nicholas II: Emperor of All the Russias* (1993; reissued 1996), is a sympathetic, detailed biography. Also of interest is Marc Ferro, *Nicholas II: The Last of the Tsars* (1991, reissued 1994; originally published in French, 1990). Andrew M. Verner, *The Crisis of Russian Autocracy: Nicholas II and the 1905 Revolution* (1990), is an authoritative study of his early reign. More popular is Robert K. Massie, *Nicholas and Alexandra* (1967, reissued 2000). The fullest study of the Romanov family's fate, based on 160 documents drawn from Russian archives, is Mark D. Steinberg and Vladimir M. Khrustalëv, *The Fall of the Romanovs: Political Dreams and Personal Struggles in a Time of Revolution* (1995). Also useful are Edvard Radzinsky, *The Last Tsar: The Life and Death of Nicholas II*, trans. from Russian (1992); and Hélène Carrère d'Encausse, *Nicholas II: The Interrupted Transition* (2000; originally published in French, 1996).

ON COUNT WITTE

Theodore von Laue, *Sergei Witte and the Industrialization of Russia* (1963), is the only study of Witte's career that is commensurate with the importance of the subject, ending with Witte's final fall from power in 1906 (includes a useful bibliography). *The Memoirs of Count Witte*, trans. and ed. by Abraham Yarmolinsky (1921), remains indispensable, though the emphasis is on Witte's career in 1905–06. *The Memoirs* in their Russian original were republished in one volume, ed. by A.L. Sidorov (1960).

ON LENIN

Dan, Theodore, ed. *The Origins of Bolshevism* (Schocken, 1970). Nation, R.C. *War on War: Lenin, the Zimmerwald Left, and the Origins of Communist Internationalism* (Duke Univ. Press, 1989). Pipes, Richard, ed. *The Unknown Lenin: From the Secret Archive* (Yale Univ. Press, 1996). Pomper, Philip. *Lenin, Trotsky, and Stalin: The Intelligentsia and Power* (Columbia Univ. Press, 1990). Remnick, David. *Lenin's Tomb: The Last Days of the Soviet Empire* (Random, 1993). Teoretik, Velikii. *Lenin: The Great Theoretician* (Progress, 1970). Volkogonov, Dmitiri. *Lenin: A New Biography* (Free Press, 1994). Von Laue, T. H. *Why Lenin? Why Stalin? Why Gorbachev?: The Rise and Fall of the Soviet System* (HarperCollins, 1993).

The most complete collection of Lenin's works is *Polnoe sobranie sochineniĭ*, 5th ed., 55 vol. (1958–65), published in Moscow; it is supplemented by his *Biograficheskaia khronika, 1870–1924*, 13 vol. (1970–85), and *Leninskiĭ sbornik*, 40 vol. in 31 (1924–85). The *Collected Works*, 45 vol. (1960–70), is a Soviet English translation of the 4th Russian edition of Lenin's works, enriched by editorial notes from the 5th edition. *Selected Works*, 3 vol. (1970–71), includes most of the works mentioned in this article and many more. Western publications of Lenin's works in English include *The Essentials of Lenin*, 2 vol. (1947, reprinted 1973), which follows the Soviet edition; and Robert C. Tucker (ed.), *The Lenin Anthology* (1975), with interpretive comments.

Biographical and critical studies include Robert D. Warth, *Lenin* (1973), an introductory study; Alfred G. Meyer, *Leninism* (1957, reprinted 1986), an analysis of Lenin's political philosophy; David Shub, *Lenin*, rev. ed. (1966, reprinted 1977), a readable and informative biography by a contemporary; Adam B. Ulam, *The Bolsheviks: The Intellectual and Political History of the Triumph of Communism in Russia* (1965, reissued 1973), a learned political biography; Bertram D. Wolfe, *Three Who Made a Revolution: A Biographical History*, 4th rev. ed. (1964, reissued 1984), a pioneering combined biography of Lenin, Trotsky, and Stalin, and *The Bridge and the Abyss: The Troubled Friendship of Maxim Gorky and V. I. Lenin* (1967, reprinted 1983); Nadezhda Krupskaya, *Reminiscences of Lenin* (1959; originally published in Russian, 1924), reticent, impersonal recollections by Lenin's widow; Leon Trotsky, *Lenin: Notes for a Biographer* (1971; originally published in Russian, 1924), an appreciation of Lenin of the Iskra period and 1917–18, the periods of Trotsky's closest collaboration with Lenin, and *The Young Lenin*, trans. from Russian (1972); Nikolay Valentinov, *Encounters with Lenin* (1968; originally published in Russian, 1953), and *The Early Years of Lenin*, trans. from Russian (1969), revealing observations on Lenin's personality by a former associate; Dietrich Geyer, *Lenin in der Russischen Sozialdemokratie* (1962), a scholarly study of Lenin and the origins of the Bolshevik-Menshevik split; Leonard Schapiro and Peter Reddaway (eds.), *Lenin: The Man, the Theorist, the Leader: A Reappraisal* (1967, reissued 1987), a collection of essays; Angelica Balabanoff, *Impressions of Lenin* (1964), by the first secretary of the Communist International; and Robert Service, *Lenin: A Political Life*, 3 vol. (1985–95).

Lenin is the subject of many historical studies, including Richard Pipes, *The Russian Revolution* (1990), and *Russia Under the Bolshevik Regime* (1993), the latter partly based on new archival sources; Harold Shukman, *Lenin and the Russian Revolution* (1967, reissued 1977); Harold Shukman and George Katkov, *Lenin's Path to Power: Bolshevism and the Destiny of Russia* (1971); Helmut Gruber, *International Communism in the Era of Lenin: A Documentary History* (1967, reissued 1972), with interpretive essays; Branko Lazitch and Milorad M. Drachkovitch, *Lenin and the Comintern* (1972); Alfred Rosmer, *Lenin's Moscow* (1971, reissued 1987; also published as *Moscow Under Lenin*, 1972; originally published in French, 1953), an insider's account of the period 1920–24, exploring the role of the party in the international Communist movement; Michael Pearson, *The Sealed Train* (1975, reissued 1989), an account of Lenin's associations with Germany and of the Russian Revolution; T. H. Rigby, *Lenin's Government: Sovnarkom, 1917–1922* (1979); and Hélène Carrère D'encausse, *Lenin: Revolution and Power* (1982; originally published in French, 1979), a study of economic, social, political, and ideological issues. Esther Kingston-Mann, *Lenin and the Problem of Marxist Peasant Revolution* (1983), emphasizes the role of the peasants in the Russian Revolution. Lenin's influence on the Bolsheviks as well as their differences are addressed in Robert C. Williams, *The Other Bolsheviks: Lenin and His Critics, 1904–1914* (1986). R. Craig Nation, *War on War: Lenin, the Zimmerwald Left, and the Origins of Communist Internationalism* (1989), explores Lenin's part in the beginnings of Communism in the 20th century.

Interpretive studies of Lenin and Leninism include Georg Lukács, *Lenin: A Study on the Unity of His Thought* (1971; originally published in German, 1924), an evaluation by a Hungarian Marxist philosopher; David Lane, *Leninism: A Sociological Interpretation* (1981); Alain Besançon, *The Rise of the Gulag: Intellectual Origins of Leninism* (1981; originally published in French, 1977); Neil Harding,

Lenin's Political Thought, 2 vol. (1977–81); Stanley W. Page, *The Geopolitics of Leninism* (1982), a critical look at Lenin's politics; and A. J. Polan, *Lenin and the End of Politics* (1984), an analysis of Lenin's politics and influence. Official Soviet interpretation of Lenin's role is provided by Boris N. Ponomarev, *Lenin and the Revolutionary Process*, trans. from Russian (1980). Nina Tumarkin, *Lenin Lives! The Lenin Cult in Soviet Russia* (1983), explores the veneration of Lenin. Further references can be found in David R. Egan, Melinda A. Egan, and Julie Anne Genthner, V. I. *Lenin: An Annotated Bibliography of English-Language Sources to 1980* (1982).

ON LEON TROTSKY

Leon Trotsky, *History of the Russian Revolution*, 3 vol. (1932–33; originally published in Russian, 1931–33), treats his own role in the third person, and *The Revolution Betrayed* (1937) is his major polemic against Stalin. Commission of Inquiry into the Charges Made Against Leon Trotsky in the Moscow Trials, *The Case of Leon Trotsky* (1937, reprinted 1968), contains Trotsky's testimony. Jan M. Meijer (ed.), *The Trotsky Papers, 1917–1922* (1964–71), contains documents from the Trotsky Archive, including the Lenin-Trotsky correspondence.

Isaac Deutscher, *The Prophet Armed: Trotsky, 1879–1921* (1954), *The Prophet Unarmed: Trotsky, 1921–1929* (1959), and *The Prophet Outcast: Trotsky, 1929–1940* (1963), constitute a classic biography of Trotsky from a sympathetic neo-Marxist point of view. Max Eastman, *Leon Trotsky: The Portrait of a Youth* (1925), is another sympathetic treatment, by a contemporary radical. Comparisons of Trotsky with fellow revolutionaries are found in Bertram D. Wolfe, *Three Who Made a Revolution* (1948), a triple biography of Lenin, Stalin, and Trotsky to 1914; and E. V. Wolfenstein, *The Revo-*

lutionary Personality: Lenin, Trotsky, Gandhi (1967), a psychoanalytic study. Robert D. Warth, *Leon Trotsky* (1977), is an introductory biography for the general reader. Biographies that depict Trotsky's brilliance as well as his shortcomings are Ian D. Thatcher, *Trotsky* (2003), an extensively researched work; Robert Service, *Trotsky: A Biography* (2009), a thoughtful and readable treatment; and Bertrand M. Patenaude, *Trotsky: Downfall of a Revolutionary* (2010), a dramatic portrait.

ON JOSEPH STALIN

The standard Soviet edition of Stalin's works in Russian is Joseph Stalin, *Sochineniia*, 13 vol. (1946–51), covering publications up to January 1934. His later works have been issued in Russian in similar format by the Hoover Institution; Robert H. McNeal (ed.), *Sochineniia*, 3 vol. (1967), is considered to be the extension, as vol. 14–16, of the standard edition. The standard edition has been translated into English and published in *Moscow: Works*, 13 vol. (1952, reprinted 1975). A selection of Stalin's works in English is Bruce Franklin (ed.), *The Essential Stalin: Major Theoretical Writings, 1905–52* (1972). An annotated bibliography, Robert H. McNeal (compiler), *Stalin's Works* (1967), considers the authenticity of material in Russian attributed to Stalin.

There is no definitive biography of Stalin. The most useful of published studies include Dmitri Volkogonov, *Stalin: Triumph and Tragedy* (1991; originally published in Russian, 1989), based on archival sources; Robert Payne, *Rise and Fall of Stalin* (1965); Leon Trotsky, *Stalin: An Appraisal of the Man and His Influence*, trans. from Russian, new ed. (1967), and *The Stalin School of Falsification*, 3rd ed. (1972; originally published in Russian, 1932), both denunciatory; Boris Souvarine, *Stalin: A Critical Survey of Bolshe-*

vism (1939, reissued 1972; originally published in French, 1935); and Bertram D. Wolfe, *Three Who Made a Revolution*, 4th rev. ed. (1964, reissued 1984). T. H. Rigby (ed.), *Stalin* (1966), is an excellent short anthology of biographical and critical material. Other studies include Adam B. Ulam, *Stalin: The Man and His Era* (1973, reprinted 1987); Ronald Hingley, *Joseph Stalin: Man and Legend* (1974); Ian Grey, *Stalin: Man of History* (1979); Robert H. McNeal, *Stalin: Man and Ruler* (1988); Robert Conquest, *Stalin: Breaker of Nations* (1991); and Alan Bullock, *Hitler and Stalin: Parallel Lives* (1991).

Reliable, detailed firsthand accounts of Stalin's domestic background are few, the only family memoirs not subject to Stalinist censorship being those published after emigration by Stalin's daughter, Svetlana Alliluyeva, *Twenty Letters to a Friend* (1967; originally published in Russian in the United States, 1967), and *Only One Year* (1969; originally published in Russian in the United States, 1969). Soviet-censored memoirs by other family members are found in David Tutaev (trans. and ed.), *The Alliluyev Memoirs* (1968).

Studies of Stalin's prerevolutionary career include Edward Ellis Smith, *The Young Stalin: The Early Years of an Elusive Revolutionary* (1967), an attempt to prove that the subject was an agent of the Tsarist political police; L. Beria, *On the History of the Bolshevik Organizations in Transcaucasia* (1949; originally published in Russian, 7th ed., 1947), the chief classic of Stalinist legend building; and, on the historical context, Catherine Merridale, *Moscow Politics and the Rise of Stalin: The Communist Party in the Capital, 1925–32* (1990); Graeme Gill, *The Origins of the Stalinist Political System* (1990); Robert V. Daniels, *Trotsky, Stalin, and Socialism* (1991); and Robert C. Tucker, *Stalin as Revolutionary, 1879–1929: A Study in History and Personality* (1973), and a sequel, *Stalin in Power: The Revolution from Above, 1928–1941* (1990).

Leonard Schapiro, *The Communist Party of the Soviet Union*, 2nd ed. (1970), is valuable on the political background of Stalin's mature career; as is John A. Armstrong, *The Politics of Totalitarianism* (1961). A more subjective version is Abdurakhman Avtorkhanov, *Stalin and the Soviet Communist Party: A Study in the Technology of Power* (1959; originally published in Russian in West Germany, 1959). Boris I. Nicolaevsky, *Power and the Soviet Elite* (1965, reissued 1975), is a collection of essays bearing on Stalin's activities from 1934 onward. Also of interest are Kendall E. Bailes, *Technology and Society Under Lenin and Stalin: Origins of the Soviet Technical Intelligentsia, 1917–1941* (1978); Eugène Zaleski, *Stalinist Planning for Economic Growth, 1933–1953* (1980; originally published in French, 1962); and Hiroaki Kuromiya, *Stalin's Industrial Revolution: Politics and Workers, 1928–1932* (1988).

Robert Conquest, *The Great Terror: Stalin's Purge of the Thirties,* rev. ed. (1973), is the fullest account of the massacres of 1937–38. Further studies are *The Great Purge Trial*, ed. by Robert C. Tucker and Stephen F. Cohen (1965), based on the official Soviet translation of the report of court proceedings; Joel Carmichael, *Stalin's Masterpiece: The Show Trials and Purges of the Thirties— The Consolidation of the Bolshevik Dictatorship* (1976); and Anton Antonov-Ovseyenko, *The Time of Stalin: Portrait of a Tyranny* (1981; originally published in Russian in the United States, 1980). F. Beck and W. Godin, *Russian Purge and the Extraction of Confession* (1951, trans. from German), remains a classic account of Stalin's reign of terror. W. G. Krivitsky, *In Stalin's Secret Service* (1939, reissued 1985; also published as *I was Stalin's Agent*, 1939, reissued 1992), is a firsthand account. Alexander Orlov, *The Secret History of Stalin's Crimes* (1953), contains informative primary sources. Nikolai Tolstoy, *Stalin's Secret War* (1981); and Adam Hochschild, *The Unquiet Ghost: Russians Remember Stalin* (1994), present testimony of victims of Stalin's purges.

ON COMMUNISM

Allan, Tony. *The Long March: The Making of Communist China* (Heine-mann Library, 2001). Berlin, Isaiah. *Karl Marx: His Life and Environment*, 4th ed. (Oxford University Press, 1996). Crossman, R. H. S., ed. *The God That Failed* (Columbia University Press, 2001). Rice, Earle, Jr. *The Cold War: Collapse of Communism* (Lucent Books, 2000). Spence, Jonathan D. *Mao Zedong* (Viking, 1999).

ON THE SOVIET UNION

Andrews, William. *The Land and the People of the Soviet Union* (Harper, 1991). Brown, Archie, and others, eds. *The Cambridge Encyclopedia of Russia and the Former Soviet Union*, 2nd ed. (Cambridge Univ. Press, 1994).Cunningham, Kevin. *Joseph Stalin and the Soviet Union* (M. Reynolds, 2006). Edwards, Judith. *Lenin and the Russian Revolution in World History* (Enslow, 2001). Gottfried, Ted. *The Road to Commu-nism; The Stalinist Empire; The Great Fatherland War; The Cold War* (Twenty-first Century, 2002–03). Medvedev, Roy. *Let History Judge: The Origins and Consequences of Stalinism*, rev. and expanded ed. (Colum-bia Univ. Press, 1989). Read, Christopher. *Lenin: A Revolutionary Life* (Routledge, 2005). Stoff, Laurie, ed. *The Rise and Fall of the Soviet Union* (Greenhaven, 2006). Streissguth, Thomas. *Life in Communist Russia* (Lucent, 2001). Suny, R. G. *The Soviet Experiment: Russia, the USSR, and the Successor States* (Oxford Univ. Press, 1998).Ulam, A. B. *The Communists: The Story of Power and Lost Illusions 1948–91* (Scrib-ner, 1992).

INDEX